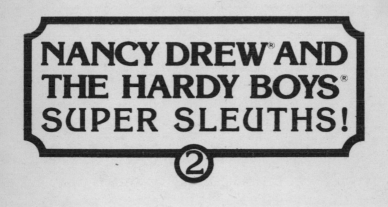

NANCY DREW® AND THE HARDY BOYS® SUPER SLEUTHS!

②

AMERICA'S THREE FAVORITE SLEUTHS TEAM UP ONCE AGAIN!

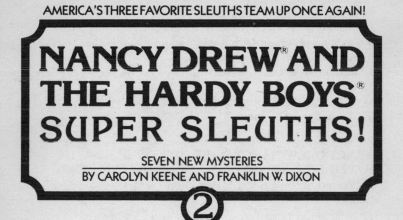

NANCY DREW® AND THE HARDY BOYS® SUPER SLEUTHS!

SEVEN NEW MYSTERIES
BY CAROLYN KEENE AND FRANKLIN W. DIXON

2

ILLUSTRATED BY PAUL FRAME

WANDERER BOOKS
PUBLISHED BY SIMON & SCHUSTER, INC., NEW YORK

Copyright © 1984 by Stratemeyer Syndicate
All rights reserved
including the right of reproduction
in whole or in part in any form
Published by WANDERER BOOKS
A Division of Simon & Schuster, Inc.
Simon & Schuster Building
1230 Avenue of the Americas
New York, New York 10020
WANDERER and colophon are registered trademarks of
Simon & Schuster, Inc.

NANCY DREW, NANCY DREW MYSTERIES and THE
HARDY BOYS are trademarks of Stratemeyer Syndicate,
registered in the United States Patent and Trademark
Office

Manufactured in the United States of America
10 9 8 7 6 5 4 3 2 1

Library of Congress Cataloging in Publication Data

Keene, Carolyn.
 Nancy Drew and the Hardy Boys, super sleuths #2.

 Contents: Old masters—Phantom thieves—A good
knight's work—[etc.]
 1. Detective and mystery stories, American.
2. Children's stories, American. [1. Mystery and
detective stories. 2. Short stories] I. Dixon,
Franklin W. II. Title.
PZ7.K23Nad 1984   [Fic]   84-5346
ISBN 0-671-50194-1

CONTENTS

FOREWORD

Dear Fans,
When we were asked to write a book of short stories in which Nancy Drew and the Hardy Boys solve mysteries, we found this a real challenge. We felt that Nancy should not grab the limelight, or Hardy readers would disapprove. If the boys stole the show, girl readers would think this very unfair. What to do? We finally decided to give these three characters equal time and let the plots develop into a collection of exciting mysteries filled with fun and wholesome adventure. We hope you enjoy them. Let us know.

C. K. and F. W. D.

OLD MASTERS

"**I** can't wait for the picture to be unveiled!" Nancy Drew whispered to her aunt.

"Neither can I," Eloise Drew said. "This Picasso is Mark's first big acquisition since he became curator of the museum. It'll establish his reputation once and for all."

A crowd had gathered around a canvas-covered painting. Nancy and her tall, attractive aunt were right in the middle of it. Just then they heard a voice behind them. "Are we late?"

Nancy turned to see Frank and Joe Hardy, her friends from Bayport, who had come to New York with her to visit Aunt Eloise.

"No," Nancy replied. "But Mark Baxter should be here any minute now to start the ceremony. I'm so excited. Who would have thought that my former art teacher would one day be in charge of a museum?"

"Well," Joe grinned, "Aunt Eloise had a hand in this, didn't she?"

Eloise Drew shrugged. "I just made a phone call. It was Mark's talent that got him the job."

Just then the curator, a tall, good-looking man with blond curly hair, walked up to the picture with his assistant, Garson Bellog, and a group of critics and benefactors.

"Ladies and gentlemen," he said. "It is my pleasure to unveil for you our newest acquisition, Pablo Picasso's *Lady and a Mirror.*"

To a round of applause, he pulled off the covering and revealed the picture. It was an abstract rendering of a woman holding a mirror.

A small, chubby man with a dark beard moved up to the picture and looked at it closely. He touched it, shook his head and touched it again.

Then he turned around and faced the crowd. "I'm afraid this Picasso is a fake!" he announced.

"What?" came shocked exclamations from the onlookers.

Mark Baxter's face turned ashen. "It can't be!" he cried out, jerking his head to stare at the painting.

"But sir, it most certainly is," the bearded man replied.

"Who is this man?" Frank whispered to Aunt Eloise.

"George Proctor, editor of *Museum World* magazine," she replied.

Proctor put his right hand on Mark Baxter's shoulder. "My friend, I have been a Picasso scholar all my life. I could tell instantly that this picture has neither the master's boldness of brush stroke nor his eye for color."

He turned to the curator's assistant, a slight man with a potbelly. "Don't you see it?"

"I do," Bellog admitted. "It's a fake, and not even a good one."

Proctor licked his finger and wiped it across the picture. Some of the paint stuck to his skin. "You see?" he went on. "It's gouache, which is water soluble, not oil as the original Picasso. How do you explain this, Mr. Baxter?"

Mark looked totally shattered. "I—I don't know," he said. "This is *definitely* not the painting I acquired. Someone must have changed it."

"Someone?" Proctor said acidly. "This wouldn't be the first time a curator perpetrated a fraud on the art-loving public so he could sell an original to a private collector for his own gain."

"That's an unfair accusation," Nancy spoke up. "You have no proof of what you say."

"Proof will be left up to the police," Proctor said. "I'm going to call them right away."

He stalked off, leaving Mark alone to face the crowd. "I—I don't know what to say," the young man stammered. "Somehow, we've been robbed!"

"What about your security system?" a man asked.

Garson Bellog shrugged. "Our security is elaborate and nearly foolproof. No one could have broken in without setting off the alarm."

An angry man shook a finger at Mark. "You'd better come up with some answers quickly, young fellow," he said menacingly.

Nancy stepped before the crowd, determined to defend the curator. "I've known Mark Baxter for many years and can vouch for his honesty. And to back it up, my friends and I will prove him innocent in this matter by finding the real thief."

"What you may find," Mr. Proctor said as he came back to the group, "is that your trust has been misplaced."

He addressed the people around the picture. "I've spoken to the police. They said that none of you may leave until you've been questioned."

"Ladies and gentlemen," Mark said, his voice quavering, "there are refreshments on the table behind you. Enjoy yourselves. I'll be in my office." He looked at Nancy and Eloise Drew.

"Do you want to talk to us?" Aunt Eloise asked.

"Please," he said. "If I ever needed friends, this is the time."

He turned and walked away, with Nancy, the

boys and Aunt Eloise right behind him. The museum was quite large, and their footsteps echoed on the polished, wooden floors. They passed white walls covered with paintings, most from the Impressionist period of the mid-1800s. Free-standing sculptures were artfully placed in several areas.

Mark's office was downstairs in a converted basement, next to a large workroom filled with easels, frames and materials. He motioned his friends to sit down, mostly on packing crates, since the office was crowded as well.

"Maybe I should have stayed in River Heights," Mark said dejectedly.

"Nonsense," Aunt Eloise scolded. "You're a talented and organized man. You're right where you belong."

"Thanks." Mark smiled weakly. "But if I can't find out what happened to the Picasso, it won't matter anyway."

"That's what we're here for," Joe spoke up. "We're going to make sure that the painting is found and returned to the museum."

His positive statement, however, did little to dissipate Mark's despair. "Ever since I began this job, there seems to have been one catastrophe after another," the young man said sadly.

"Like what?" Nancy asked.

"Mysteriously cancelled deliveries . . . minor

vandalism . . . even a few threats."

Frank's eyebrows shot up. "What kind of threats?"

"Anonymous phone calls," Mark said, "telling me to get out of New York, to go back where I came from if I know what's good for me. Stuff like that."

"But why?" Nancy asked.

"I'm an outsider. A lot of people here don't seem willing to accept me. You saw the way Proctor treated me today."

"Well, you'll just have to prove them wrong," Aunt Eloise said firmly.

"When was the last time you saw the Picasso?" Frank wanted to know.

"Yesterday afternoon," Mark replied without hesitation. "I covered it myself for the official ceremony today."

"We'll need a list of all the people who have been here between then and now," Nancy said.

"Make two of them," came a voice from the doorway.

They turned to see Mr. Bellog walk up with a man in a rumpled suit.

"Detective Morgan," Garson Bellog introduced his companion. "From the police."

"We've already checked out your security system," the officer said. "It's operating just fine."

Mark shrugged. "I can't imagine how the

painting got out of here, then."

"Maybe it didn't," Frank stated.

"Who are you?" Detective Morgan asked.

"Frank Hardy. And this is my brother, Joe, and our friend, Nancy Drew."

Mark spoke up. "I've asked Nancy and the boys to help me with my own investigation. They're amateur detectives."

The man nodded. "What's this about the Picasso not leaving?"

"Well," Frank said, "if security's still intact, perhaps someone switched paintings, planning to remove the original later."

Detective Morgan scratched a mole on his chin. "You mean the thief might have hidden the painting somewhere in the museum itself?"

"Right."

"We'll search the place after interviewing the people upstairs," the detective declared. "Mr. Baxter, I want a copy of the list you're making up, and I want to tell you now: don't leave town without letting us know exactly where you'll be."

"Am I a suspect?" Mark asked.

"Everyone's a suspect," Mr. Morgan said and walked out of the room.

"Mr. Fisher stopped me upstairs," Bellog spoke up.

"Who's he?" Frank inquired.

"Chairman of the board," Aunt Eloise replied.

Bellog continued. "Most of the board members are here now. While they were waiting for the police to arrive, they had a meeting discussing this unfortunate loss." He turned his eyes to the floor. "Mark, they feel it would be best if you were to resign from your job until the investigation is finished and everything is straightened out."

"Do I have to clear out of the office?" Mark asked.

"Yes," Bellog replied softly. "Look, I'm really sorry about the turn things have taken."

"Thanks, Garson," Mark said. "You've been a good friend and a good assistant. Who will be in charge in my absence?"

Bellog hesitated. "They—asked me," he said, "but I'm thinking about turning them down."

"You'll do no such thing!" Mark objected. "I can't think of anyone I'd rather have in charge than you."

"All right," Garson Bellog said, a slight smile passing his lips. "If you insist, I will take the job."

"Will we be able to conduct our investigation with Mark gone?" Nancy asked.

Garson Bellog nodded. "Of course. I'll help you with anything you want if it will clear Mark's name."

The Leicock Museum, named for the endowment left by its chief benefactor, was located on East Fifty-eighth Street, just a few blocks from Central Park. After Nancy and the boys had been questioned by the police and were free to leave, they said good-bye to Mark and Aunt Eloise and headed for the park to enjoy the spring weather and discuss the case. Frank had the list of possible suspects that Mark had prepared.

The young detectives purchased Italian ices from a street vendor, then sat on a bench in the shade of a big elm tree.

"Do you think they'll find the painting hidden in the museum?" Nancy asked.

"I don't know," Frank answered.

"What about that list?" Joe asked.

Frank pulled it out of his pocket and glanced at the names. "Mark and Mr. Bellog are on it, of course, and several workmen and art students," he said.

"Art students?" Joe said.

Nancy shrugged. "Bellog worked at the place when it was only a small gallery. He still teaches classes in the basement."

"It doesn't sound very promising," Joe said thoughtfully. "The part that doesn't make sense is the forgery. Did the forger think his painting was really going to fool people?"

"That's what puzzles me, too," Nancy added. "Why bother to copy a Picasso and do it badly? And to use water-based paint when the original is done in oils? The texture's not even the same."

"What *is* the difference?" Joe asked.

"Gouache is more opaque," Nancy said. "Even an untrained eye can tell the difference when the two are put side by side."

Frank sighed. "It's really crazy."

"And it's about to get crazier," Joe said, pointing. "Look!"

Down the path from their bench, two men were standing close together, talking.

"Isn't that Mr. Bellog?" Nancy whispered.

"Yes," Frank answered. "And the man with him seems to be that Proctor character from *Museum World*."

"Let's see if we can get close enough to hear what they're saying," Joe suggested.

The amateur sleuths stood up and strolled away from the path until they came to a stand of trees. The men were just on the other side.

"They're walking away," Frank whispered, disappointed.

Indeed, Bellog and Proctor went down the path and entered the small Central Park Zoo, where jugglers and street musicians worked their magic to entertain the visitors.

"It'll be impossible to get close to them now without being seen," Frank said.

"Maybe not!" Nancy was looking at a man in a clown costume who carried a gaggle of helium balloons in his hands. "I have an idea."

She approached the clown, who had a stark white face decorated with a big red nose that looked like a cherry on a sundae.

"Excuse me," Nancy said.

"There's no excuse for you," the clown answered in a high voice before doing an exaggerated silent laugh. "What can I do for you?"

"My friends will buy all your balloons if you'll do us a favor," Nancy replied.

Frank nudged her. "Your friends?" he asked.

"I didn't bring any money with me," Nancy returned in a low voice.

Joe rolled his eyes, while the clown stared at them, wondering what he had gotten himself into. "What is it you want?" he asked.

Nancy, smiling prettily, laid out her plan. A minute later the clown was walking into the zoo, Nancy in step right behind him. The boys were on either side of him, holding several balloons in front of their faces so they would not be recognized.

Bellog and Proctor had stopped in front of the monkey cage and were talking animatedly.

"Get as close as you can without letting them

know we're listening," Nancy whispered to the clown.

He grunted and moved nearer the men.

"I think you're right," the sleuths heard Bellog say. "He's always talking to me about private collections of stolen paintings, and how much they're worth."

"He's an outsider," Proctor returned. "I never trusted him when I heard where he came from."

"I think he did the forgery himself," Bellog declared. "Something that looks that crass is about par for his talent."

That comment stung Nancy. She had nothing but the greatest respect for Mark's abilities as an artist ever since he taught her painting in high school.

Both men laughed, then Bellog put a hand on Proctor's shoulder.

"Don't you dare quote me on any of this."

"Don't worry," the editor said. "We'll call you an informed source. But keep me posted on what's happening."

"Sure will," Bellog replied, then both men walked off.

Frank paid the clown for the balloons and handed them to Nancy.

"I feel like I've lost twenty pounds." She giggled.

"What are you going to do with them?" Frank asked.

"Aunt Eloise is a teacher," Nancy returned. "I'll give them to her to take to school for the kids."

"That Bellog sure is a troublemaker," Joe said. "He tells Mark how sorry he is, then tries to stir it up with that editor."

Nancy nodded. "I wonder about how much of Mark's 'trouble' is a direct result of Bellog's meddling."

"You know," Frank said, "Bellog stands to gain a great deal if Mark is fired. He's already been put into Mark's job."

"Do you think that he had anything to do with the disappearance of the painting?" Joe asked.

Nancy shrugged. "He's on the list of suspects, and he certainly had a motive."

"But we need proof!" Frank declared.

"Where do we start looking?" Joe asked.

No one had an answer. The young detectives took a bus to Aunt Eloise's apartment, anxious to hear if the police had any luck finding the Picasso in the museum, or if they uncovered any important clues to its whereabouts.

When they walked in, Mark was sitting on a long, white brocaded sofa talking to Aunt Eloise, who sat cross-legged on the floor.

"Let's not mention our feelings about Mr. Bellog yet," Nancy told the boys at the door.

"Right," Frank agreed. "If we accuse anyone without proof, we're no better than Proctor."

21

Nancy's balloons caused a minor stir. When the business of what to do with them was settled, the girl turned to the matter at hand.

"Have the police uncovered anything?" she asked.

Mark shook his head sadly. "They searched the entire building, top to bottom, and are convinced that the painting is not there. Yet, they can't explain how it was taken out."

"Tell me about the security procedures," Frank said.

Mark sighed. "Each painting is protected by an alarm that goes off if anyone tries to take the picture off the wall. That same alarm, when it is activated, locks every door and window in the building. The doors and windows are jimmy-proof and unbreakable, besides being connected to the alarm system."

"Who controls all this?" Joe asked.

"I do," Mark answered. "There's a master control board that operates from one key. Before I left yesterday, I double-checked to make sure everything was turned on."

"Do you still have the key?" Nancy asked.

"I had to turn it over to Garson when I cleared out today."

Nancy and the boys exchanged glances.

"I suppose you were the last one to leave last night?" Frank asked.

Mark nodded. "I was working in the office when Garson came in and told me he was going home. A bit after that, I walked through the building, checked the new Picasso one more time, set the alarm, then went out."

"Does the museum employ security guards?" Frank inquired.

"No," Mark answered. "We spent all our money on the alarm system."

The evening passed glumly. Even after going to bed, Nancy could not sleep. In the middle of the night, she got up for a glass of milk and a piece of chocolate cake they had had for dessert. It may not help me sleep, she thought, but it'll certainly make my staying awake more enjoyable!

She heard noises in the kitchen when she arrived and found that Frank and Joe had been thinking along the same lines.

"Pull up a chair," Joe invited her.

"We're discussing the impossible," Frank added.

Nancy nodded and sat at the large butcher-block table, pouring herself a glass of milk.

"How," Frank asked, "do you sneak a forgery into a museum, switch it for a genuine Picasso, then walk out with the real thing without disturbing any alarms or breaking any windows or doors?"

"You forgot the biggest question of all," Nancy added. "Why not just steal the picture? Why bother to replace it with a fake that will fool no one? The answer to that, I believe, will give us the answers to all the other questions."

"Nancy's right," Joe said. "That's the key that will open all the doors. We just have to find it."

Nancy swallowed before commenting. "Tomorrow we go back to the museum. Maybe we'll find something the police overlooked."

Next morning bright and early, the three young sleuths were knocking on the locked door of the Leicock Museum. A sign hung above it, saying CLOSED UNTIL FURTHER NOTICE.

After several minutes a surprised Garson Bellog came out. "What do you want?" he asked suspiciously.

Nancy smiled. "We're here to start our investigation, Mr. Bellog. Remember, you offered your help yesterday?"

Bellog nodded reluctantly and slowly opened the door. "But stay out of the way," he said. "You can't take too long, either, because we're still moving things around to get ready to reopen. Besides, it would be . . . dangerous for you to stay here too long. I wouldn't want you to get hurt."

"Don't worry," Joe said. "We can take care of ourselves."

They walked right past the man and into the room where the picture had hung. It was gone.

"Where's the forgery?" Nancy asked.

Bellog, who had followed the group, grimaced. "Locked in the downstairs office," he said. "We didn't want anything to happen to it. It's evidence, you know."

"Thanks," Nancy said. "We'll just poke around a little on our own."

"If you need anything, ask me," the man muttered, then wandered off.

A few painters and workmen moved casually around the museum, but they were hardly a safety hazard for Nancy and the boys.

"If I'd have known about the cold reception Mr. Bellog would give us," Joe said, "I'd have worn an overcoat."

"I'm becoming more and more convinced that he's involved in this theft," Nancy declared. "He certainly seems to like being in control."

The detectives examined the spot where the painting had hung. They saw where the alarm wires came through the wall and had been snipped to break the connection.

"It looks as if the alarm system ran right through the picture frame," Frank stated. "I don't know how anyone could have gotten the Picasso away from the wall without setting off the bells."

Joe was kneeling on the floor, his fingertips brushing lightly over the polished surface. "Something's down here," he said.

Frank and Nancy crouched beside him and felt the floor. Little spots, like tiny bumps, were scattered beneath the spot where the painting had hung. They were so small that they could hardly be seen, and it was difficult to determine what color they were.

"They look like . . . paint splatters," Frank decided.

"That's it!" Nancy confirmed.

She licked a finger and rubbed the floor with it. Then she stood up. "I must see the forgery— right away."

"Well, let's go down and ask Mr. Bellog," Joe suggested.

"No," Nancy returned firmly. "I don't think he'll show it to us."

"Why not?" Frank asked.

"I'll tell you after I've seen it," she replied teasingly.

"You drive a hard bargain," Joe said, but he had an inkling of what his friend was up to.

They quickly devised a plan and went down the long staircase to the basement. They found the office door closed, but could hear someone moving around inside.

Nancy quickly pulled several student easels

together in the workroom and slipped behind them. When she was well hidden, the boys pounded on the office door.

"Mr. Bellog! Mr. Bellog!" they yelled excitedly.

Bellog opened the door a crack and looked angrily at Frank and Joe. "What is it?"

"I think we've found something!" Frank said, his breath shallow, as if he had been running.

"Yes," Joe added convincingly. "You'll have to come, quick!"

Bellog stared at them for several seconds, then stepped out of the office, and pushed the button to lock the door. Nancy wasn't surprised.

The three hurried upstairs. As soon as their footsteps had disappeared into the gallery, the girl jumped up and ran to the door.

She opened her purse and rummaged in it until she found her laminated River Heights Library card. She slipped it into the crack between the door and the frame and pushed on the locking mechanism. The door sprang open!

In the office, she saw the fake Picasso in its beautiful gold frame set up on an easel. Next to it stood another easel, holding a picture that was covered with a drop cloth.

Nancy pulled off the cloth and gasped. She was looking at another copy of *Lady with a Mirror*. A close examination with a wet finger revealed to the young detective that this was a second forgery, and not the original. Nancy smiled.

In the gallery Mr. Bellog stooped to the floor and examined the paint drippings.

"What do you think?" Frank asked him. "Perhaps this is a big clue?"

The curator pursed his thick lips. "Probably not," he said. "We've had workmen in here for weeks painting the walls and ceilings. It's just their drips."

"We never thought about that," Joe said, disappointed.

The man stood up, straightening his tie. "I will call this to the attention of the police, though," he said, smiling thinly. "You never know." Then he turned to leave. The boys followed. At the door, they met Nancy.

"Did you have any luck?" she asked sweetly.

"Naw," Frank said. "I thought we did, but it turned out to be nothing."

"Well, we'd better be going," Nancy said. "We need to tell Mark the bad news."

"It's a shame things are going so badly," Bellog said, sounding truly concerned.

"A real shame," Nancy repeated.

As soon as he had ushered them out of the museum, Nancy said, "We have to make some phone calls!"

"What's the story?" Frank asked.

"I'm not sure yet," Nancy returned. "But I think we're very close to solving the case of the missing Picasso. One of us needs to stay here, though, to see if Bellog leaves."

"I'll do it," Joe said.

"Great," Nancy replied. "But keep out of his view. If anything drastic happens, call us at Aunt Eloise's."

Joe hid in a doorway across the street, and Nancy and Frank went back to the apartment, where Nancy made several phone calls. Then she and Frank waited through the afternoon, uneasily watching the clock. At six fifteen, Joe called to say that Bellog had just closed the museum and left for the night.

"Did he have a package with him?" Nancy inquired.

"As a matter of fact, he did," Joe answered.

"Good. Stay there. We'll be along shortly."

Aunt Eloise, who had returned from school earlier, drove Nancy and Frank to the museum. Joe was sitting on the outside steps, waiting for them.

"I'm glad you're all here," he said. "What happens now?"

"We're not *all* here yet," Nancy corrected. Just then, Lieutenant Morgan walked up to the group with a tall, white-haired man.

"This is Mr. Fisher, the chairman of the board of directors of the Leicock Museum," the police officer introduced his companion.

"Thank you for coming," Nancy said. "Did you manage to turn off the alarm, Mr. Fisher?"

The distinguished-looking chairman smiled. "It took some doing. I hope this is as important as you say it is."

"So do I," Nancy agreed.

"Hi, everybody!" The young detectives whirled around to see Mark Baxter. And with him was the editor of *Museum World*, Mr. Proctor!

"You've taken me away from a delicious dinner!" Proctor growled. "It better be worth it."

Nancy just smiled. "Shall we go in?"

Mr. Fisher opened the door. It was dark inside the museum.

"The lights are over here," Mark said, reaching for the switch.

"No!" Nancy cautioned. "Leave them off."

In the faint gleam of her pencil flashlight, she led the way to the main gallery. Bellog had hung up the fake Picasso again, though it wasn't hooked up to the alarm this time.

"Now what?" Proctor grumbled.

"Now we wait," Nancy said.

"How long?" Detective Morgan asked.

"I don't know . . . ssh, what's that?" the girl whispered.

"Someone's coming through the door," Mark said.

"Quick, everybody hide," Nancy urged, and the group hurried into the adjoining room, watching through the doorway as a figure crept in and walked up to the forgery. Nancy eased herself toward the light switch, and when the intruder reached for the picture, she turned on the lights.

The furtive visitor, who was Garson Bellog, gasped. His hands seemed to be stuck on the painting as he stared at the group on the doorway in utter shock. A package lay at his feet.

"You're under arrest!" Detective Morgan snapped.

"What are you talking about?" Bellog asked angrily. "I belong here. *You're* the interlopers." Then his eyes lit on Mr. Fisher and his face turned ashen.

Nancy walked up to the painting. "Here is the real Picasso," she said.

"No, it's not!" Proctor declared. "It's the forgery! Just look at it."

"No," Nancy corrected. "Look *under* it."

With that she wet a handkerchief with her tongue and wiped over the paint. The water-soluble gouache began to come off, revealing the identical colors beneath—in oils.

"I don't believe it!" Proctor cried out.

"The reason the alarm never went off is that

the picture was never removed," Nancy explained. "Mr. Bellog painted right over it two nights ago."

"But he couldn't have!" Mark said. "Remember, I was the last one out, and I checked the Picasso before I left."

"That's right," Bellog said angrily. "I demand an apology, and want you all out of my museum right away!"

"Did you actually see Mr. Bellog leave the building, Mark?" Frank asked.

"Actually, no," Mark replied. "He *told* me he was going. I just assumed . . ."

"You don't have anything on me," Bellog rasped. "You can't prove . . ."

His voice trailed off when Nancy bent down and picked up the package at his feet. "We know that Mr. Bellog had the most to gain by Mark being discredited," the young sleuth went on. "He wanted to be curator himself, and resented Mark for getting the job. But by forging the Picasso, he could have it—and more!"

"That's mine!" Bellog cried, and reached for the package.

"It's evidence," Nancy said, and quickly handed the parcel to Lt. Morgan.

"Bellog told Mark he was leaving," she continued, "then hid in the workroom. When Mark went home, Bellog hurried upstairs with his gouache and painted over the Picasso, using the real painting as his guide. Then he spent the rest of the night somewhere in the museum. In the morning, he simply 'showed up' for the unveiling."

Bellog glared at her, but Nancy went on, undaunted.

"Step one was complete. Mark was discredited. Then came step two. Knowing that the police would take the fake Picasso for evidence, he had to make sure he got the valuable painting beneath it. He made another forgery for the museum so he could take the original home."

Frank snapped his fingers. "Then he could wash off his paint job and have a genuine Picasso."

"Which he could sell to an unscrupulous private collector later on," Proctor added.

"Right," Nancy confirmed.

"So he got Mark's job," Joe spoke up, "and stood to make a fortune by selling the Picasso."

"But I don't understand why he came back tonight," Detective Morgan said. "He could have taken the picture home when he left the museum!"

"He did," Nancy said. "But when I found the second forgery in the office today, I put it into the gold frame, then set the first forgery with the original underneath on the easel. Mr. Bellog,

33

thinking things were just the opposite, switched the pictures back."

"You mean he put the fake with the original underneath into the frame and took the worthless forgery with him?" Proctor exclaimed. "What a story!"

"That's right" Nancy agreed. "When he got home and wiped off the gouache, he realized he had the wrong picture. So he packed it up and brought it back here. She unrolled the package, revealing the second forgery. "I knew we'd have an airtight case if we could catch him in the act of switching. That's why I invited all you people to come here and wait for him."

"Great case!" Detective Morgan cried out. "It's ironclad! You've done a wonderful piece of detective work," he added with a smile.

"Thanks," Nancy said.

Mr. Proctor walked up to Mark and put out his hand. "I've been wrong before," he said, "but never this wrong. My humblest apologies."

"It's okay," Mark said, beaming. "Just give us a fair review in *Museum World*."

"You can depend on it."

Detective Morgan put a pair of handcuffs on Garson Bellog and read him his rights.

"What made you recognize Garson's scheme, Nancy?" Mr. Fisher asked the young detective.

"We found paint drippings on the floor under the picture," Nancy explained.

Frank grinned. "Mr. Bellog said they were from the workmen who painted the gallery. But the ceiling and walls are white, and the drippings, even though it was hard to tell, were light blue!

PHANTOM THIEVES

Nancy Drew pulled the parka hood tightly around her reddish-blond hair and turned her face from the driving rain.

"I don't think it's ever going to stop!" the amateur detective said to her friends Frank and Joe Hardy, who sat on the bench behind her in the aluminum fishing boat.

"It'll stop all right," said the National Guard officer next to her. "The question is: will we have a city left when it does?"

Their boat was moving along what had once been Independence Boulevard in Jackson. The fall rains had come, forcing the Ohio River over its banks, and now Independence Boulevard was six feet underwater.

"Colonel Drew," Joe Hardy asked the National Guard officer, who was a distant relative of Nancy's, "what are the latest weather reports?"

The man's pleasant face was creased by tension. "It's supposed to start breaking up by 8 A.M.," he replied. Then he looked at his watch. "It's 6 A.M. now."

"How long before the waters will begin to recede?" Frank inquired.

The colonel shrugged. "A couple of days at least, I'm afraid. Even after the rain has stopped, it will take a while for the flood waters to crest and then subside."

"Which means there's plenty of time for more looting," Nancy said worriedly.

Another fishing boat putted up beside them out of the pre-dawn shadows. Several National Guardsmen were huddled in it.

"Colonel Drew," one of them called out, "we have a problem over on Fifth Street."

The colonel groaned. "Not Henvy's Department Store again!"

"Yes, sir!" the man answered.

"Looting?"

"Right. And Mr. Henvy is raising the roof, sir!"

Colonel Drew nodded tiredly. "Tell Mr. Henvy that we're on our way," he said.

"Yes, sir!" the soldier said and saluted. Then he turned to his colleague who was operating the motor of the boat. "Let's go." A moment later, they slid away.

Colonel Drew looked at the young detectives.

"Three straight days of looting, and I'm powerless to stop it. We had half the National Guard out here in boats last night, and yet the crooks sneaked into Henvy's place again."

"Don't blame yourself, Uncle Chris," Nancy told him. "Since martial law was declared, you've evacuated the citizens, kept them sheltered and fed, and maintained order. You should be proud of all you have accomplished."

The colonel smiled. "Thanks, Nancy," he said. Then he played the beam of the searchlight out over the still, dark waters. "We'd better get over to Henvy's."

Frank reached back and started the outboard. It moved slowly through the watery passages between brick buildings, while Colonel Drew shone the light ahead so they wouldn't run into anything. Jackson was an eerie sight, like a ghost town springing up out of a river.

The sky had lightened considerably by the time they reached the department store. Boats full of soldiers dotted the waterscape in all directions, while Mr. Henvy, owner of the store, stood on the deck of a small pontoon skiff with a fringed canopy.

Frank drew up alongside it.

"I see you and your soldier boys have been helping yourselves to our stuff again," Henvy said angrily to Colonel Drew.

The colonel looked at him sharply. "Slander is against the law in this country," he said.

"Well, who else could be doing it?" Henvy demanded, his chubby face set in a scowl. "You tell me you're going to watch my building, and I get ripped off for the third straight day."

"What's missing this time?" Joe asked.

"So far, all the silverware," the man returned. "Bob and Roy, my sons, are assessing the damage now. When the water goes down, I won't have anything left to sell."

"Let's go in," the colonel said.

The front door was nearly underwater, but there was a fire escape leading up the side of the building.

Frank pulled up to the stairs that dipped into the water. A guardsman was stationed on the lowest rung. He saluted.

"Were you on duty last night?" Colonel Drew asked him.

"Yes, sir! I was here all the time."

"No one got into the building over the fire escape?"

"No, sir!"

"Ask him if *he* did it!" Mr. Henvy demanded, as his skiff moved to the metal structure.

Colonel Drew ignored the remark. "It was quiet last night?"

"Like a grave," the soldier confirmed.

"Let's go in," the colonel repeated and stepped onto the stairs. "Bring the flashlights, Joe."

Joe grabbed the waterproof sack full of flashlights and climbed out of the gently rocking boat, his parka slicking water. Frank and Nancy were right behind him.

The door was open when they reached the top of the slippery stairs. Because of the flooding, all the electricity was out, and the building was enveloped in darkness.

"I don't get it," Joe said to the colonel. "Your men were watching the store last night, weren't they?"

"Five boatloads," the officer replied. "They had nothing to do but to keep an eye on this place."

Joe handed out the flashlights, and a moment later, slender beams crisscrossed in the darkened store.

"There's light coming from that far corner," Nancy noted. "Henvy's sons must be there."

"Let's see what they've found," Colonel Drew said.

The group picked their way through the furniture section to the houseware department. Bob and Roy Henvy, both heavyset and in their thirties, were taking inventory under their flashlight beams.

"Why do the looters pick on us?" Bob complained when everyone walked up. "There are other stores in town."

"And how do they come in?" his brother added.

"Well, I'm getting my gun," Bob declared, "and stand watch from now on myself. Nobody's going to break into this place anymore."

"Protecting your property is my job," Colonel Drew said sternly. "You will have to observe the curfew like everyone else."

"Then why don't you do your job?" Bob demanded loudly.

"What's missing this time?" Nancy asked.

"Nothing much," Roy said sarcastically. "Just about thirty-thousand-dollars' worth of silver."

"You're insured, of course," Frank interjected.

Bob Henvy shrugged. "What good does the insurance do? In two or three days, when the water goes down, we'll need the merchandise. Otherwise we'll lose our customers."

"Let me post a guard *inside* tonight," the colonel said.

"No," Roy objected. "This is *our* property, and we're not going to have someone we don't know roaming around in here. We suspect it's your people doing the stealing anyway."

"Mind if we look around a bit?" Frank asked.

"Of course we mind," Bob replied. "We don't want strangers taking advantage of us."

"This is Nancy Drew and the Hardy brothers," the colonel pointed out. "They're amateur detectives, and very successful ones at that. Perhaps they can find a clue that will help solve this mystery."

The Henvys looked at each other. "Well," Roy shrugged. "Maybe they can help."

"Worth a try," Bob agreed.

Colonel Drew smiled at Nancy and her friends. "Good luck," he said.

Then the group wandered off.

"I'm afraid we won't find much in the dark," Nancy spoke up after a few moments. "I'm not even sure what we should look for."

"It seems to me," Frank said, "that we should try to figure how the looters got in and out without being seen."

"Apparently they didn't come up the fire escape," Joe said. "And there are no windows except on the first floor, which is underwater."

"Let's go down as far as we can," Frank said. "Maybe we'll get an idea."

They made their way carefully down a non-working escalator. The flood covered the first floor, coming up halfway to the ceiling. Nancy and the boys sat on the last dry step and played their lights through the water.

"There's no merchandise here at all," Joe said in surprise.

"When the water began to rise," Nancy told him, "Henvy had his employees carry everything to a higher level."

Frank shone his light toward the display windows. They had been broken from the pressure of the rising flood.

"You could certainly get through there," he said, "if you could hold your breath long enough."

"Or if you had scuba gear," Nancy added.

"Scuba gear!" Frank repeated. "That may be the answer! The looters could swim under the guards' boats, slip through the windows and go upstairs. There they could take their time stealing things, put them in big sacks and leave the way they came. No one would be the wiser."

Joe spoke up. "If we blocked off those windows somehow, the looters wouldn't be able to get in anymore."

"But we couldn't catch them that way either," Nancy said. "They'd just go somewhere else and do the same thing."

"Right," Frank agreed. "So what do we do?"

"We could check around town and see if anyone's been buying compressed air," Nancy suggested. "And there might be a scuba club, too, where we could ask questions."

"We should also lay a trap in case the culprits return to this store tonight," Joe said. "I hope they do."

"I don't see why they wouldn't," Nancy said. "No one has stopped them before, and there's still plenty of merchandise for greedy thieves."

"It's worth a try," Frank agreed. "First, let's go back to Colonel Drew's house and check the phone book for suppliers of oxygen. Then we'll have to figure out a way to get there, since the phones are not working."

The young detectives left with Colonel Drew, moving past a scowling Mr. Henvy in his pontoon boat. The rain had indeed stopped, but as the colonel had predicted, the weatherman expected the waters to crest sometime the next day before subsiding.

Colonel Drew dropped Nancy and the boys off at his home, then returned to his duties. The house was just outside of the city and on a high enough hill so that the waters didn't reach it.

The colonel's wife, Edith, greeted the group at the door with three hot mugs of cocoa.

"How did you know that's what we needed?" Nancy said, giving the petite, black-haired woman a loving hug.

"Lucky guess," Edith Drew replied. "I suppose dry clothes would be appreciated, too."

The young people couldn't have agreed more. After they had changed and enjoyed the cocoa, they sat on the floor by the warming fireplace and went through the phone book.

"This isn't exactly a great scuba-diving city,"

Joe said after a few minutes.

"Too far away from the water," Frank returned. "But that should make our job easier."

They found nothing listed under "scuba," so they tried "sporting goods."

"Wait—here's something," Nancy said. "Granite Lake Emporium, everything for the fisherman, skier, and diver."

"Granite Lake?" Frank asked.

"It's not far from here," Nancy explained. "It's an old quarry with a rock bottom, so the water may be clear enough to do some diving."

Joe riffled through the phone book. He found a listing for an organization called the "Wet Suit Club."

"That's here in Jackson," he said. "But it'll take a boat to get there."

"How about Granite Lake?" Frank asked.

"It's on a higher elevation," Nancy returned, "and can be reached by car."

"Maybe we ought to split up," Joe suggested. "You drive up to the emporium in your aunt's station wagon, Nancy, and we'll take a boat downtown to see if anyone is at that club."

"Good idea," Nancy agreed. "We'll keep in touch via CB radio. There's one in the car and in Uncle Chris's boat. Aunt Edith told me he should be home soon; his shift ends in about five minutes if things are going according to schedule. I'm sure he'll let you use the boat."

Within the hour Nancy was driving Edith Drew's station wagon into the parking lot of the Granite Lake Emporium. It was a large log building with a blue neon sign.

The proprietor, a grizzled little old man, stood behind a well-worn counter when she entered.

"Nice day for fish," he said cheerily.

The place seemed to be a conglomeration of grocery items and sporting goods, with merchandise jammed into every nook and cranny.

Nancy smiled. "Guess you're not getting much business today."

"You're the first," the little man said. "Outside of my phantom customers."

Nancy walked up to him and put out her hand. "My name's Nancy Drew," she said.

The man greeted her warmly. "I'm Easy Hollis," he said, "and that's how I live—easy. You kin to Colonel Drew?"

"Yes," she returned. "Did you say something about phantoms?"

"My scuba phantoms." Easy grinned. "I've been filling their air tanks."

Nancy's ears perked up. "Why do you call them phantoms?" she asked.

"'Cause I never see 'em, that's why," Easy replied. "For the last three days, when I open up in the morning, there's a couple of tanks waiting by the door with money taped to 'em. When I close at night, I put 'em back out on the porch full up, and then they're waiting for me with money again in the morning."

"Who would want air tanks at night?" Nancy asked.

Easy smiled wide, showing missing teeth. "Phantoms," he said.

"There it is!" Joe said, pointing to a large frame house, the first story of which was partly underwater. "That's the address."

Frank switched off the engine. Another boat was moored to the porch railing. He bumped up next to it and tied up the same way.

"Hello!" he called out. "Anybody home?"

An athletic-looking man in his twenties poked his head out of a second-story window.

"Welcome to my river-front property," he replied, smiling broadly. "What can I do for you?"

"I'm Frank Hardy," Frank introduced himself, squinting into the now sunny sky. "This is my brother, Joe. Is this the Wet Suit Club?"

"I'll say it is," the man answered. "Except it's more like the Wet Floor Club now. I'll be right down."

He appeared within a minute, wading through knee-deep water onto the porch. He wore fisherman's boots that came all the way up to his waist. "Must be something pretty important to bring you out on a day like this," he said. "I'm Red Flanders, president of the club."

"We're amateur detectives on an investigation," Frank explained. "Would you mind if we asked you a few questions?"

Flanders shook his head. "I don't mind a bit," he replied. "It will give me the chance to delay cleaning up this place, which my wife wanted me to do."

"We won't take very long," Joe said.

"Too bad," Red joked, sliding a hand through the rust-colored hair that was obviously the source of his name.

"Do you keep a membership list of everyone who belongs to the club?" Frank asked.

Red bent over the rail, leaning his elbows on it. "Sure," he said. "Why?"

"We were just wondering if we could have a look at it," Joe said casually.

The man stared at them for a moment, obviously curious. "It's not a large club," he said. "And since we don't have any clear water here, we do most of our diving at Granite Lake."

"Is the list handy?" Frank persisted.

Red Flanders smiled. "Maybe and maybe not," he said. "It's in the filing cabinet, which is on the first floor. Part of it's underwater and part's above. If it's in the top drawer, I can get it for you. If it's in the bottom drawer, the best I can give you is a soggy wad of paper."

"Fair enough," Joe said.

"I'll go look," Red offered.

"You certainly seem to be taking all this in your stride," Frank remarked.

The man shrugged. "I may as well laugh about it. It's a lot more fun than crying and complaining, which won't change the situation anyway."

He waded into the house.

The CB radio in the boat crackled to life. "Frank? Joe? This is Nancy. Over."

Frank picked up the microphone and pushed the button on its side. "This is Frank. Go ahead, Nancy. Over."

"I have good news and bad news," she said. "The good news is that I've found where our looters are refilling their tanks. The bad news is that the owner has never seen them. They leave the air tanks by the door with their money, and pick the tanks up at night after he's filled them with oxygen. Over."

"What time does the store usually close?" Frank asked.

"At five," Nancy returned. "I think I'll stay around a while and see what develops. Over."

"Roger," Frank said. "We're trying to get hold of the club membership list. We'll let you know what we find. Take care. Over."

"Great!" Nancy responded. "If you can't raise me on the radio, it means that I'm inside talking with Easy Hollis, the owner of the store. He says he has a lot of interesting stories for me. Over."

Frank grinned. "Well, get a good earful," he said. "Over and out."

"Sounds like Nancy's found a friend," Joe remarked, as Frank replaced the microphone.

Before Frank could comment, Red sloshed out the front door. "You're in luck!" he announced, holding up a piece of dry paper. "The list was above water."

He handed it over the wooden rail, and Frank began to scan about twenty names.

"This contains everyone?" he asked.

The man nodded. "Everyone who's ever dived with us."

Frank's eyes stopped about two-thirds down the list. "Look at this," he said to Joe, handing his brother the paper.

Joe stared at the list. "It's too much to be a coincidence," he murmured.

Frank grunted and turned to the red-headed scuba diver. "Bob and Roy Henvy are on the list," he said.

"That's 'cause they're in the club," Red returned.

"Are they good divers?"

The man pursed his lips. "Only because they have good equipment. They take the best stuff out of the sporting goods department of their store and use it. They like the deep water because they have high-wattage lights for where it's really dark."

"Mind if we borrow the list?" Frank asked.

"You can keep it," Red said. "I have another copy. Besides, after this flooding, everyone in town will want to join the club, so we'll have to make a new one anyway."

The boys thanked the good-natured man, and then putted off. Frank tried to raise Nancy on the radio, but couldn't reach her.

"I don't like this," Joe said. "Suppose the Henvys are doing all the looting?"

"It makes sense in a strange way," Frank said. "They could steal their own stuff, hide it, then resell it later after the insurance has paid them off. Jewelry has been robbed, fur coats, expensive tools—to say nothing of the silver. They could stand to make several hundred thousand dollars, I figure."

Joe nodded. Then a look of concern came over his face. "I'm worried about Nancy," he said. "The Henvys know who she is. And if they spot her when they come to get the tanks, who knows what they'll do!"

"I'll try and reach her again," Frank said tensely.

He spoke into the radio, but to no avail. "What now?" he said with concern.

"We can't just sit here and wait," Joe decided.

"You're right," Frank agreed. "Let's go back to the Drews' and see if we can borrow the colonel's car to get Nancy."

"Good idea," Joe said, and they headed the boat out of the city.

Nancy had listened to Easy's stories of strange occurrences on the lake for several hours and would have enjoyed hearing more, but five o'clock arrived, and the little man wanted to close up shop.

"Looks like I could have stayed home today," he said. "I didn't sell a thing."

"There will be other days," Nancy replied. "Thanks for helping me pass the time."

"The pleasure was all mine," he answered. "It can get kinda lonely around here."

"You're sure it's okay for me to stay outside and watch for a while?" she asked.

"Fine with me," Easy said. "I'd like to know who those phantom fellers are myself."

They walked out the door, and Easy Hollis locked it, after tucking an umbrella under his arm. "I live about two hundred yards down that road," he said, pointing at a dirt incline that led to the lake. "If you need anything, come on over!"

"Thanks, Easy," Nancy said, and the man sauntered off.

The young detective walked to the station wagon and climbed in. She turned on the CB.

"Joe or Frank, come in. This is Nancy. Over." She waited, but there was no reply.

"Come in, Frank. Come in, Joe," she urged. "You guys were supposed to stand by! Over." Nothing but static came back.

"It's beginning to get spooky out here," she added, half to the microphone, half to herself. Nancy was concentrating on the radio and didn't hear the black van that had pulled into the parking lot until it was almost beside her.

Suddenly, she turned her head and found herself staring straight into the mean, dark eyes of Bob Henvy!

He realized instantly why she was there, and Nancy felt a chill going down her spine. She jammed her key into the ignition and started the car, hoping to get away. But the Henvy's van was already running. As soon as Bob saw that Nancy was trying to escape, he put the van into reverse and squealed straight back. Then he pulled up again, this time right behind the station wagon's back bumper!

Nancy was trapped! The building was in front of her, and the van was blocking her in the rear.

A second later the men jumped out of the van. Bob came for Nancy, while Roy, who had been in the passenger seat, ran up to the store and grabbed the oxygen tanks.

The girl had had enough time to lock all the doors in the wagon before Bob reached her. He pounded angrily on the windows. "Come out right now!" he screamed.

Nancy grabbed the mike. "Joe! Frank! It's the Henvys. The Henvys. Please help me!"

She looked up just in time to see Roy Henvy lift one of the heavy oxygen tanks and throw it at her window.

Frank and Joe Hardy didn't hear Nancy's cries for help because they were in the house, receiving directions from Edith Drew on how to get to the Granite Lake Emporium.

"Do you think I should wake Chris?" she asked. "He's catching up on his sleep."

"He needs to rest," Frank said. "We'll be okay as long as we have the car."

"That's no problem," Edith said. "Ferdie Deering next door is in the guard, too. Chris can get a ride to work with him if you're not back by then."

"Thanks," Frank said, and took the keys to the colonel's blue Pontiac.

Edith wished them luck in finding Nancy and gave each of them a sandwich. Then they hurried out the door.

"Grab the radio," Frank said.

Joe got the radio out of the boat, which stood on a trailer in the driveway. Quickly, he hooked it up to a connection in the car. Then Frank drove off.

"Try Nancy again," he said between mouthfuls of bread.

His brother nodded and took the mike. "Nancy, this is Joe. Over. Nancy, please respond. Over."

Silence. "It's after five," Frank said worriedly. "She should be sticking close to the radio by now."

They drove to the Emporium as fast as the speed limit allowed and arrived just as the sun was setting behind a wooded hill. Edith Drew's station wagon was there, and a small man was standing beside it.

"What's going on?" Joe asked and got out of the Pontiac.

"I don't know," the man said sadly. "Are you Frank and Joe?"

"Yes," Frank said. He pointed to the broken window of the station wagon. "What happened?"

"I heard screaming," the man replied. "So I hurried up here as fast as I could, but they were already gone. By the way, I'm Easy Hollis, the owner of the store."

"Those crooks got Nancy!" Joe exclaimed. "I bet they've taken her with them!"

Frank looked at Easy Hollis. "Can we rent some scuba gear from you?"

"Rent? No," Easy replied. "But you can sure have whatever you need!"

"Thanks, Mr. Hollis," Frank said, and they all hurried into the store. Hollis didn't have underwater lights, but he had aqua flares that would help somewhat. The boys took the gear and quickly drove back to Jackson.

"What if we run into the guard?" Joe said, after they had parked at the edge of the flooded area and gotten into the gear. "Should we explain everything?"

"No time," Frank responded. "Every second could be precious. We'll go into Henvy's quietly, just as Roy and Bob did."

"I hope they're in there."

Frank pulled his tank strap tight. "They've got to be," he said resolutely.

The young detectives checked the air gauges on their tanks and stepped into the water. The wet suits kept out the fall chill.

Carefully, they pulled the release on the first of their flares, then dove down, entering another world.

The flares glowed brightly underwater, but still only illuminated a small area around the divers. The Hardys had to move slowly and cautiously as they glided through the deserted streets of the flooded city.

It took several flares before they found Henvy's Department Store. They passed beneath a number of National Guard boats that were pulled up close to the building. The colonel was taking no chances, Joe thought. A moment later the boys had slipped through a broken window.

They surfaced to eerie darkness. The only light was the reddish glow of the exit lights, which ran on dry cell batteries.

Suddenly, they heard a voice, gurgling hollowly in the cave-like room.

Frank pulled out his mouthpiece. "Nancy!" he called. "Nancy!"

"Frank!" Nancy returned. "I—" Then her voice was choked off.

"Over there!" Joe said, and pointed to the far end of the room. There, a figure was struggling, bobbing in the water.

The boys swam quickly toward Nancy, trying to avoid display cases and clothes' racks.

They reached her as she went almost underwater. Joe pulled her up by the arms.

"My foot," she choked out. "They've tied my foot!"

"I'll take care of it," Frank called and dove down. He touched Nancy's ankle, but couldn't clearly see it. It was fastened by a thick rope to a checkout counter.

Working tensely, he untied her at last, then came back to the surface.

"It's the Henvys," she gasped, gulping air. "They're doing this looting themselves, they . . ."

"We know," Joe said. "Just take it easy. Let's get out of here."

All at once, a bright light was shining on them.

"There!" came Bob Henvy's voice from the escalator. He was training a powerful underwater spotlight on the group. "Get them!"

"Let's go!" Frank yelled, then looked at Nancy. "Hold on to me!"

He pulled the tab on a flare and dove, just as the Henvys jumped in after them.

The young detectives went down, making their way through the maze of counters, kicking for the windows. Joe turned and looked behind. The Henvys' powerful lights were dim, glowing spheres closing in on them.

Frank pulled the mouthpiece from between his lips and let Nancy use it for a few seconds before taking it back.

The lights were drawing nearer to them as they made it through the window and went for the surface. They popped out to stare into the faces of several National Guardsmen led by Colonel Drew.

"What are you doing here?" the colonel asked incredulously.

"It's the Henvys," Frank said, as someone offered him a hand. "*They're* the looters, and they're after us now!"

The guardsmen pulled the young people into their boat.

"I see lights!" a private called suddenly, pointing.

Sure enough, below the surface two glowing spheres were moving erratically through the water.

"The Henvys are taking off!" Nancy called.

"We'll follow them," Colonel Drew decided. "I have a feeling that those birds are going home to roost."

The boat trailed the glowing balls through the streets of Jackson, while Nancy and the boys told their stories to Colonel Drew. The officer seethed with anger when he heard the final, threatening episode.

"You could have drowned, Nancy!" he cried out. "That water is still rising."

Nancy nodded. "I almost did. Good thing the boys—"

"Stop here," Frank interrupted tensely, as they were about to round the corner of a building.

Colonel Drew cut the engine and glided silently around the bend. Mr. Henvy's pontoon boat was hidden in an alley between two buildings.

The group watched as the lights below them approached the boat. When Mr. Henvy reached down and started pulling his sons up, the guard closed in.

"I see you're out after curfew," Colonel Drew called to the surprised store owner, who was lifting Roy and a rubber sack out of the water. Gasping, Roy let go of the sack, and watches spilled all over the deck.

"So what?" Henvy said defiantly.

"So you're under arrest!" the colonel said. He and his men climbed onto the deck of the pontoon boat.

"For what?" Henvy demanded, pointing to the watches. "This is *our* merchandise from *our* store! You can't arrest me for trying to save my own stuff!"

"We'll charge you with breaking the curfew," Colonel Drew said. "Then we can talk about a major fraud perpetrated against your insurance company. To that we can add attempted murder. Sorry, Mr. Henvy. You and your sons are going away for a long time."

Henvy suddenly realized that his game was over. He sat down on the wet deck and buried his face in his hands. "I always have all the rotten luck," he whined.

"Not always," Nancy said, climbing on deck. "You had a wonderful business until you decided to break the law."

Bob and Roy stared at the girl detective, then

at their father, who was being handcuffed. "I can't believe we were caught because of a couple of nosy kids!" Roy fumed. "We had such a perfect scheme!"

"Crime is never perfect," Frank said.

A GOOD KNIGHT'S WORK

The afternoon sun shone brightly on the medieval fair that was taking place in Bayport. Frank Hardy and his friend Nancy Drew were enjoying themselves as they strolled among the laughing and singing crowd.

They had just stopped at a gaily decorated booth when two men dressed like knights of King Arthur's round table marched up to them. Joe Hardy, Frank's younger brother, followed behind, a big smile on his face.

"What are the king's colors?" one of the men demanded of Frank and Nancy.

"The what?" Frank looked puzzled.

"If you don't know the answer, I'm afraid you'll have to come with us," the knight declared. Then he and his companion took Frank and Nancy by their arms, and led them away from the booth.

"Joe Hardy!" Nancy called over her shoulder, "I have a feeling *you're* responsible for this!"

Joe chuckled but did not reply. The two young detectives were brought to the stocks and directed to bend over and put their heads and hands into the designated slots. Then the wooden top of the device was lowered, trapping them inside!

"This is uncomfortable!" Frank complained.

"We'll let you out in two or three years," Joe intoned solemnly.

"You'll get us out of here in about five seconds!" Nancy demanded.

Their captors grinned. "What are the king's colors?" they asked again.

Frank glared at his brother.

"Purple and gold," Joe whispered.

"Purple and gold," Frank repeated. "Now let me out of here. I'm getting a backache!"

Laughter rippled through the crowd as the knights hurried to free the captives. And by the time the stocks were lifted, Frank and Nancy were joining in the merriment.

The pretty, titian-haired girl turned to Joe, who wore the costume of a medieval knight. "Do not think you have heard the last of this, you blackguard," she said, adopting the language of the Middle Ages.

"Milady, you do me wrong," Joe responded. "I was merely protecting the honor of the king."

Suddenly, they heard a loud groan from

among the onlookers. There was excited chatter, as a man in a business suit staggered through their midst, moving erratically, his eyes glazed.

"Something's wrong," Frank said, and the young detectives rushed toward the man. However, he fell to the ground before they reached him.

Frank lifted the stranger's head to cradle it. "What's the matter?" he asked anxiously.

"Someone get a doctor!" Joe shouted, and several people ran off in different directions.

The man looked up at Frank, his eyes having difficulty focusing. "It's a . . . dark night," he said weakly.

"What?" Nancy said, putting her ear near his mouth.

"It's a . . . dark night," the stranger repeated. Then his eyelids fluttered and he went limp.

Nancy checked his wrists. "He's unconscious," she said, "and his pulse rate is very low."

"I think I know what caused it," Frank declared. He pointed to a large knot that was forming on the back of the man's head.

"He sure got himself a nasty bump!" Joe said.

"Or someone *gave* him a nasty bump," Nancy added. "Let's see if his money was stolen."

Frank reached into the man's inside coat pocket and pulled out a black cowhide wallet. He opened it, exposing several bills and a large, brass-colored badge.

"He's a policeman!" Nancy exclaimed.

"Detective Sergeant Michael Mayo," Frank read from the man's ID card. "Bayport Police Department. I wonder what happened?"

A large crowd, talking in whispers, had gathered around the fallen officer.

"Excuse me. Let me through, please!" A man dressed in motley, like a court jester, pushed his way through the onlookers toward Nancy and the boys. He carried a small black bag.

"I may look like a fool, but I'm really a doctor," he said, and bent down to the man to take his pulse. Then he examined the patient's head.

"Something or somebody really hit him hard," the doctor commented. "He may have a concussion. Has anyone called for an ambulance?"

Frank stood up. "I'll do it," he volunteered. "And I'll call the police, too. Detective Mayo was probably on duty when he was hurt."

Within ten minutes the craft fair was swarming with squad cars. One of them escorted the ambulance that carried Detective Mayo and carefully made its way over the rough terrain of the fairground.

Chief Collig, an old friend of the Hardy family, stood with the boys and Nancy and watched the ambulance leave.

"I hope he'll be all right," Nancy said.

"Me too," Chief Collig replied. "And I hope he regains consciousness quickly enough to tell us what happened so we can pursue his attacker."

"Then you think it was definitely a case of assault?" Joe asked.

"I know it was," Chief Collig replied grimly. "Perhaps the three of you can help us. I'm glad Nancy's here to visit. The more people I have, the better."

"We'll be glad to do anything we can," Frank offered.

"Good," the chief nodded. "You see, earlier this week, we received word that a prisoner named Jess Wallace had escaped from the Federal Reformatory at nearby Seneca. He was seen heading into our jurisdiction. We sent Mike into the field to check out the reports."

"But why would Wallace come here?" Nancy asked.

"Well, he has family in Bayport," the chief answered, "and we have to be thorough. We've been watching all the places where we think he might hide, but haven't spotted him yet."

"Why did Detective Mayo come to the fair?" Joe asked.

"He was checking on Wallace's cousin, Jerry, who lives nearby," Chief Collig replied. "Maybe Jerry came here. We don't know. It's really difficult to be sure with all the activity going on."

A uniformed police officer approached the group, towing a man dressed in plaid pants and a green shirt.

"This is Jerry Wallace," the policeman said.

Chief Collig stared at Wallace. "Why'd you hit our man on the head?" he asked brusquely.

Wallace laughed. "You can't pin that on me," he replied. "I've been over at the battlefield watching the jousts."

"Since when are you interested in things like this?" the chief asked suspiciously.

Wallace shrugged. "I was getting tired of TV," he said curtly. "Besides, it's a free country."

"Check out his story," Chief Collig told the policeman. "If it clicks, we'll have to let him go."

"Yes, sir."

The officer left with Jerry Wallace, and the chief, a tall, ruddy man, focused his eyes on the young sleuths. "We've posted a man in the parking lot to watch all cars. If you're planning to stay here a while, will you keep an eye out for this Wallace character?" He pulled a small photo from his pocket and showed it to the amateur detectives. "Jess Wallace is about five feet eleven inches tall and weighs 180 pounds," he added.

"Do you really believe he's here?" Joe inquired.

The chief shrugged. "I *don't* believe Detective Mayo's blow on the head was accidental or coincidental. Somebody hit him, and it wasn't to steal his wallet. You add it up."

"You know, Mr. Mayo said something before he passed out," Nancy remembered. "He said, 'It's a dark night.'"

"If I were blacking out, I'd probably say the same thing," Chief Collig mused. "That's it?"

Nancy nodded.

"So, our job is to stay here," Frank stated.

Chief Collig smiled. "Stay here, enjoy yourselves and keep your sharp eyes open."

"Sounds like an easy assignment," Joe commented and straightened the chain mail on his chest. Then the young people said goodbye to the chief and moved on.

"What's the name of the organization you belong to that runs this fair?" Nancy asked Joe.

"The Society for Creative Anachronism," he replied proudly. "We call it SCA for short."

"And everyone dresses up in costumes from the Middle Ages?"

"There's more to it than that," Joe said. "SCA is a highly-organized national group. We belong to what is called the East Kingdom. We have our own hierarchy that has a king and lots of other ranks, incuding knights like me and peasants as well. Everyone in the society adopts an alter ego. You become someone who lived between the time of the Fall of the Roman Empire to 1600."

"And you have a fair every year?"

"Yes. It's a chance for us to get together in our alter egos," Joe said. "We sell crafts that are handmade and have jousts and other contests. Today is a special day, by the way."

"Why's that?" Nancy asked.

"Our king, Darius Maximus of the Holy Roman Empire, is stepping down from his throne," Joe said. "We will be choosing a successor on the field of honor this afternoon."

He put a hand to his chest. "That successor will be me," he went on dramatically. "All I have to do is vanquish the bravest knights of the kingdom."

"Maybe you can *talk* them into submission," Frank quipped.

Joe gave his brother a withering look.

"What's your SCA name?" Nancy went on.

"Sir Siegfried the Wingfoot. I am a Bavarian knight of the fourteenth century."

"Oh, brother!" Frank groaned.

Nancy giggled. "It sounds pretty funny. Tell me, Sir Siegfried, could you escort us to the battlefield?"

"Follow me," Joe said. "I have need to go there anyway."

They moved through the fair. It was as if they had walked into a time machine and come out in the days of beautiful damsels and dashing knights in shining armor.

"If this is the Middle Ages," Nancy said, "and we're the lords and ladies, I suppose that makes Jess Wallace the mean old dragon."

"Let's hope he doesn't breathe fire," Frank joked.

They passed leather and woodwork booths that smelled clean and fresh, then stopped for several minutes to listen to a wandering troubador. By the time they arrived at the field of honor, the tournaments had already begun.

They walked up to the roped-off ground where two knights were harmlessly dueling with mock swords and shields. "Sir Siegfried!" a tall young man called out to Joe. He was wearing a golden crown and a yellow goatee.

"Your Majesty," Joe said, going down on one knee and bowing his head.

"Rise, knight," the king said, and Joe stood up.

They shook hands. "I've been wondering where you've been hiding," the king said.

"We had a little excitement before," Joe explained, then made the introductions. "This is

His Highness, Darius Maximus, also known as Eric Porter," he said to Nancy.

"A pleasure," King Darius said, staring admiringly at the pretty girl detective.

"Iola's been looking for you," he then said to Joe. "She's ready for you to become king so she can be your consort."

"What do you think of the competition?" Joe asked.

The king shrugged. "You know most of the club members," he said. "But there are a lot of walk-ons today that I don't know much about."

He indicated a line of knights sitting in the front row of the makeshift grandstand on the far side of the green field.

"I've met some of them," King Darius went on. "The one with the sunburst shield is really a girl. The Black Knight over there is a fellow named Denny who's been camping out here since before the fair. . . ."

"I'll meet them on the battlefield," Joe said.

"Do you feel lucky today?" asked a girl behind them. They turned and saw Iola Morton walk up. She was wearing a long satin gown with puffy sleeves. Her pixie face looked radiant under the long braids of dark hair that were wound around her head.

"Iola, you look beautiful!" Nancy exclaimed.

"You'll make a regal queen!" Joe added.

"When do you enter the tournament, Joe?" Frank asked. "I can't wait to see who gets to thrash my little brother."

"We draw lots to see who faces whichever champion is on the field," Joe responded. "It isn't my turn yet."

"Well, I'd better go back to the royal box," King Darius decided. "My subjects will be missing me. Good luck, Sir Siegfried."

"Thank you, your Majesty," Joe responded, as the king walked to the special enclosure from where he would officially sanction the beginning of each new round.

"Let's watch for a while," Nancy suggested.

They all sat on the ground by the rope, rather than in the grandstand. The two knights were still fighting, but one of them was beginning to tire and back away.

"What are the swords made of?" Nancy asked.

"Rattan wood covered with duct tape," Joe replied. "The shields are made of plywood. The knights' armor is heavy leather."

"How do you know when someone wins?" Frank asked.

"It's an honor system," Joe explained. "If you think you've been struck a fatal blow, you admit defeat."

Nancy giggled. "How chivalrous."

"I concede!" called the knight who had been

tiring, and a cheer went up from the crowd.

"Look over there," Nancy suddenly whispered, and pointed to the grandstand. "Isn't that Jerry Wallace?"

"He's still here," Frank said. "Apparently the police had to let him go."

"We honor the winner!" the king called from his special box. "Sir Vlad Ravna!"

Everyone applauded as the knight who wore a peaked helmet held his sword in the air.

But the young detectives paid little attention. Instead, their eyes were riveted on the man with the plaid pants.

"He's getting up," Frank said. "Let's follow him."

"Uh-oh," Iola said. "I smell sleuthing afoot."

"Chief Collig did tell us to keep our eyes open," Nancy said, and quickly filled Iola in on what had happened earlier.

"I have to stay for the tournament," Joe declared. "You go on ahead."

The king raised his hands for silence from the crowd. Dipping his hand into a bowl full of paper slips, he drew one out and read from it. "The next challenger, from parts unknown, is the Black Knight!"

A man strode onto the field, his clothes and leathers dark, his helmet tightly fixed onto his face with only the eyeholes visible. He was the

Black Knight from fiction, the embodiment of evil. And he played his part well, shaking his fist at the crowd, who loudly booed in disapproval.

Frank and Nancy stood up as Jerry Wallace disappeared behind the grandstand.

"Good luck," Joe said.

"Same to you," Nancy said and gave her friend a quick hug. Then she and Frank walked away, letting Jerry Wallace stay a distance ahead of them as they moved through the large crowd.

"He seems to be going toward the parking lot," Frank said.

Nancy nodded. "Maybe the police will follow him if he tries to leave."

The parking lot was a clearing in a grove of trees. It only had one combination entrance and exit, situated at the far end. A black and white squad car was parked in a spot from where every car that left or entered could be watched.

Wallace moved away from the path and into the trees as he neared the lot.

"He's trying to avoid being seen by the police," Nancy said. "I wonder why?"

Frank shrugged. "Let's stay on the path," he said. "It will give us a good view of the whole area."

They walked on quickly, then stopped behind a clump of shrubs.

"There he is," Nancy whispered.

The suspect was ducking behind a row of cars that were backed up to the tree line.

"He's definitely trying to stay out of sight," Frank said. "Now he stopped. What's he doing?"

"I can't see him well enough to tell," Nancy said.

Jerry Wallace was crouching low behind a green sedan. All at once the trunk popped open, and he rooted around inside.

"*What* is he doing?" Frank repeated, frustrated that he could not see.

Wallace stayed low for a while, then stood up, looking all around. It forced Nancy and Frank behind the trees to avoid detection.

When they peeked out again, the man was crouching behind a brown Chevy.

"Should we alert the police?" Nancy asked.

"And ruin the chance of catching the man's cousin?" Frank returned. "Let's just watch a bit longer. We can call the police if he tries to get away."

Jerry Wallace stayed low behind the car for a moment, then hurried back to the sedan with the open trunk. Once again he crouched, doing something the young detectives could not see. Then he stood up and shut the trunk.

"Whatever he was up to, I think he's finished," Frank whispered.

At that point the man turned away from the lot and retreated into the woods!

"He's going back to the fair!" Nancy said.

"Let's follow him," Frank said, and the two started up the path. Finally, Jerry Wallace came out of the woods a distance ahead of them.

They trailed him to the area where SCA members were camping for the weekend. Wallace stopped in front of a high-peaked, red and white striped tent. He stuck his right arm through the flap, then withdrew it and walked on!

"What was that all about?" Nancy asked, puzzled.

"I don't know," Frank replied. "And look, now he's walking off into the woods!"

Sure enough, Jerry Wallace turned away from the fairgrounds and was heading into the surrounding forest.

"Should we follow?" Nancy asked quickly.

"I think it's time to tell the police what's going on, if they don't already know."

"Right," Nancy agreed, and the two hurried to the parking lot.

On the battlefield a knight in green leathers tumbled to the ground. He had received an illegal blow on the back of the knees from his challenger, the Black Knight, who put the tip of his wooden sword near his victim's neck. It was the Black Knight's third straight victory, and he hadn't fought a fair fight yet!

"The next challenger," the king called out, "will be Sir Siegfried the Wingfoot."

Joe sprang to his feet. He picked up the helmet that lay beside him on the grass.

"Good luck," Iola said and kissed him on the cheek.

"I'll need it if that guy keeps fighting dirty," Joe grumbled and put on the thick leather helmet. He took his shield, which had an eagle with bared talons on its crest, and strode onto the field. The Black Knight was waiting, hands on his hips.

"I've been watching you," Joe told him when he got close. "You don't play fair. If you foul me, you'll get the same thing back!"

Instead of responding, the Black Knight lashed out with his sword. Joe was barely able to deflect the blow with his shield.

"We haven't officially begun!" the king admonished. But the Black Knight struck again!

This time Joe was ready for him. He took the blow fully on his shield and responded with a series of small slashes that caught his opponent just below his shield.

The Black Knight grunted and came back with several shots across Joe's shins. Yet, hits below the knee were illegal!

The onlookers cried out in protest.

Meanwhile, a uniformed policeman stood in the parking lot, looking at the suspicious green sedan Frank and Nancy had pointed out to him.

"Wallace opened the trunk," Frank said, "fiddled around for a while, then went to . . . this other car."

They walked to the brown Chevy and looked it over.

"I don't see anything," the policeman said. "What in the world was he doing?"

Just then his colleague came up to them. "Headquarters is sending someone to Jerry Wallace's place to pick him up," he reported. "And we've got help coming here, too, just in case."

"Any word on Mr. Mayo?" Nancy asked.

"I talked with Chief Collig," the officer returned. "The doctors told him that Mayo was still unconscious, but that he'd be all right."

"I hope so," the girl said. "Now, do you want to see the tent Wallace stuck his arm in?"

The policemen nodded. "Sure. You show us the way."

They all went to the camping area and stopped at the tent with the red and white stripes.

One of the officers put his head inside, then pulled back. "No one's in there," he said.

"What now?" Nancy asked.

"I think Roger here and I are going to separate and look around," the policeman answered.

"Okay," Frank said. "We'll keep our eyes open, too." He and Nancy wandered around the tent.

"There has to be an explanation for this," the Hardy boy mused.

"Let's find out whom the tent belongs to," Nancy suggested. "Maybe Jerry Wallace pitched it out here himself." .

They went to the other campers to make inquiries. Finally, they discovered that the striped tent belonged to one of the teenaged SCA members.

"What now?" Frank asked.

"Let's look inside," Nancy said. "Wallace stuck his arm in there for a reason."

Frank thought for a second, then shrugged. "Why not?" he replied, and they entered the canvas structure.

It was warm in the tent with no circulating air. In one corner stood a cot. Next to it was a large chest with a lock on it. Various weapons and tools were lined up on the walls.

"Not much here," Frank commented.

"Let's look around carefully," Nancy advised. "Perhaps we'll find a hidden clue somewhere."

The two worked silently for a few minutes, then Frank suddenly held out something with a shout of triumph.

"What's this?" Nancy asked.

"A car key," the boy replied. "I found it under the cot!"

"No one would deliberately keep his key under a cot," Nancy declared.

"But someone could have tossed it there," Frank returned. "Someone like Jerry Wallace!"

"I have an idea," Nancy said. "Let's go back to the cars."

Taking the key, the two left the tent and hurried down the path to the parking area. They ran to the green sedan whose trunk Wallace had opened.

"Keep your fingers crossed," Nancy said, and slipped the key into the lock. It worked!

A moment later Frank and Nancy were staring into the trunk. A spare tire lay inside, along with a small toolbox containing various screwdrivers and wrenches. Otherwise, the compartment was empty.

"Now what?" Frank asked.

Nancy smiled. "Now this," she said. She reached into the toolbox and extracted a screwdriver. "I tried to put Wallace's actions together and could only come up with one explanation. Look here."

She motioned for Frank to squat behind the car with her. "There," she said, pointing to the license plate. "Look at how the dust has been disturbed around the screws."

"He used the screwdriver to remove the license plate!" Frank exclaimed. "That means he probably switched plates with that brown Chevy."

"Right."

"There could only be one reason," Frank went on. "His convict cousin is here at the fair, and Jerry has left his car for him. He switched plates so that the police can't trace it, then threw the key into that tent. . . ."

"But why that particular tent?" Nancy wondered. "Do you think that its owner is in cahoots with him?"

"Either that, or its owner is a prisoner of Wallace."

"But where would Jerry have taken him?"

"The chest!" Frank cried out. "Maybe Jerry stuffed him into that chest!"

"Let's get back to the tent," Nancy said. "Hurry!"

They ran all the way to the camping site and rushed into the striped tent. Nancy flew over to the large chest and rapped on it with her knuckles.

There was no response.

She banged on the container with the heel of her hand, then put her ear to the wood. Just then she heard a weak moan.

"We'll have to open this!" she decided.

Frank looked at the tools lined up on the wall. He grabbed a hammer.

"Good," Nancy said. "Hit the lock."

Frank swung out and pounded the strong lock. After several blows the mechanism gave way, and they were able to open the chest. Inside, a teenage boy lay bound and gagged.

Quickly, the young detectives lifted him out of the chest, and Nancy removed his gag.

"He tied me up," the boy rasped. "Put me in there this morning. Took my gear, too."

"Who are you?" Frank asked.

"What?"

"What character?" Nancy persisted.

"Oh," the boy replied weakly. "I'm the Black Knight!"

Out on the field, Sir Siegfried and the Black Knight traded blows in equal measure. The knight not only played unfairly, but he seemed to have little understanding of the sport. His lack of experience kept Joe in the contest. The Hardy boy's skill evened out his opponent's brute force.

Then the knight's attention wandered for an instant to something just off the field. A policeman was walking by!

Joe took the opportunity to get around his adversary's guard and strike a decisive blow to the back. The knight stumbled, but regained his balance.

"That was a fatal blow," Joe declared. "You must concede!"

But the knight responded with another strike that drove his young challenger back.

Suddenly, an idea clicked in Joe's mind.

"Dark night," he said, while he and the Black Knight circled each other. "Detective Mayo said, 'It's a dark night.' "

The knight swung wildly at him, but missed.

"He didn't know the correct title," Joe went on. "If he had said Black Knight, we would have understood right away. You're the escaped convict, Jess Wallace!"

The man charged him once again, trying to finish him off, but Joe sidestepped and caught his adversary on the back.

"Since your cousin Jerry's house was being watched, you posed as the Black Knight, hoping Jerry would supply you with money and transportation to cover your tracks."

The convict came at him again, but Joe parried easily. "Detective Mayo was too clever for you and figured it out, so you conked him." At that point, the athletic young detective landed several blows on the man's head, causing him to stagger.

"You were planning to hide out at the fair until the pressure was off. But it's not going to work."

Suddenly, there was a commotion among the onlookers. A number of policemen were rushing toward the battlefield.

"Looks like you're out of time *and* luck!" Joe finished.

His adversary darted his head frantically, then dropped his shield and began to run. Joe chased the man, who by now was exhausted, and used the sword to trip him. Then he jumped on Jess Wallace.

"Do you yield?" he demanded.

"Yes, yes," the bogus Black Knight said wearily.

The police crowded around, and Chief Collig took Jess Wallace into custody.

Just then, Nancy and Frank came up with the real Black Knight they had rescued from the chest. Quickly, they told their story to Joe and a smiling Chief Collig.

"I want to thank all of you," the chief said. "You've done a tremendous job." He shook hands with the young detectives, when another officer arrived.

"We caught Jerry Wallace at his house," he reported. "And we've heard from the hospital.

Mayo is awake and doing fine. He said to tell you that it's the Black Night."

Everyone laughed.

King Darius Maximus came forward and put a hand on Joe's shoulder. "I've been conferring with my advisors," he said. "It was decided that you, Sir Siegfried, will be named the new King of the East Kingdom for meritorious valor on and off the field of battle."

A cheer went up from the crowd, and Iola hugged Joe.

"Not so fast," Nancy warned. She had left the group unnoticed and now returned with the two knights who had put her in the stocks earlier. "This man is under arrest." She pointed to Joe.

"What?" Joe stared at her, open-mouthed, as her companions took him by the arms. "What's the charge?"

"Unchivalrous behavior," Nancy declared. "You had Frank and me put into the stocks today for insufficient reasons. It was humiliating."

"But I'm the king now!" Joe objected.

"Not until you've served your sentence," Darius Maximus announced. He winked at the two knights and raised his arms ceremoniously. "Take him away!"

"We'll see you in two or three years," Nancy

called, as they led Joe to the stocks, and the crowd's laughter followed him all the way across the field.

PURGE

"I 'm afraid you'll have to come with us,"
the police officer said, resting his hand
on the shoulder of a tall, gray-haired
man.

"Do you have to take him *now*?" Carson
Drew asked. The famous lawyer and father of
Nancy Drew looked around the crowded lobby
of the River Heights Bank. Then his gaze went
back to the gray-haired man. "Mr. Slayton has
been a respected officer of this institution for
many years. Can't you spare him the embar-
rassment of arresting him in public?"

"I'm sorry," the policeman apologized. "But
my orders are to take Mr. Slayton to headquarters."

"Could he ride with us?" Nancy suggested.
"We promise to bring him right in."

The pretty, titian-haired detective just
couldn't believe that Alistair Slayton was guilty
of anything. He had been a close friend of the
family's for years.

"It's all right," Mr. Slayton spoke up, and came around the desk he had occupied for nearly twenty years. "I'll go with him. He's just trying to do his job. Do you need to handcuff me, officer?"

The policeman shook his head. "That won't be necessary."

"What's the charge?" Frank Hardy inquired. He and his brother, Joe, were in River Heights to visit the Drews during Christmas vacation and had accompanied their friend, Nancy, and her father to the bank after an urgent call from Mr. Slayton had interrupted their lunch.

"Embezzlement," the policeman said. "Over three million dollars are missing from the bank. And Mr. Slayton, the treasurer, is charged with the crime."

By now all activity around them had stopped. Customers and employees were watching the group with tense curiosity.

Mr. Slayton's eyes were moist as he looked at Mr. Drew. "Guess I'll be needing a lawyer," he said softly.

"You've got one," Mr. Drew answered. "Me."

"Then I've got the best."

Mr. Slayton shook hands with Mr. Drew, Nancy and the boys.

"All right," he then told the policeman, "I'm ready."

"As soon as they set bail, we'll have you out," Mr. Drew promised him as he was led away. "And don't worry. This must be a misunderstanding."

Mr. Slayton, who looked pale and defeated, smiled weakly. A moment later he was gone. Nancy turned to her father. "He couldn't have done what they accused him of," she said angrily.

"I know, honey," he answered and put an arm around her. "It hurts me to see him taken away like that, too."

"Can't you do anything?" Joe asked.

Mr. Drew shook his head. "He'll have to appear before a judge in the morning for arraignment, where it'll be decided whether or not there is enough evidence to charge him. If so, bail will be set. We can't get him free until then."

"What kind of proof could they possibly have against Mr. Slayton?" Nancy asked.

A voice spoke up behind them. "Very damaging proof, I'm afraid."

Malcolm Tobey, the bank's president, had walked up to the group together with a younger man in a dark, pin-striped suit. "I wouldn't have believed it," Mr. Tobey went on, "but the evidence is irrefutable."

"What sort of evidence?" Nancy repeated.

"We don't need to tell you anything," the younger man replied. "Being friends of an embezzler doesn't entitle you to any special information!"

Mr. Tobey turned to him. "Mr. Drew and Nancy are good friends and good customers," he declared, his voice sounding tired. "You should treat them with more respect." To the Drews he said, "This is my nephew, Dennis Johnson."

"My apologies," Johnson stated, but the words did not come easily.

"Perhaps we could all go into my office and discuss this privately," Mr. Tobey suggested.

Mr. Drew nodded. "I'd appreciate it."

A few minutes later they were seated in the bank president's walnut-paneled office, where an accountant with horn-rimmed glasses joined them. He carried a large ledger.

"This is Mr. McCain, the government auditor," Mr. Tobey introduced him.

The man with the ledger book shook their hands. "I've heard of Carson and Nancy Drew and the Hardy boys," he said.

"And we've heard of the government," Frank returned with a smile, breaking the tension for a moment and making everyone feel more comfortable.

"I suppose we should start at the beginning," the president said. "Mr. McCain can do a better job than I can."

The auditor nodded. "Every bank insured by the federal government must have its records examined each year to ascertain that all the money is where it's supposed to be," he began. "I started my audit last week, checking the cash on hand, investments, loans and losses. The figure I came up with is three million dollars higher than those the bank reported."

"That's a lot of money," Nancy said. "Are you sure?"

The man shrugged. "A bank's finances can get pretty complicated. We'll have to break down all the investments and loans for last year one by one to see where the problem lies."

"But what makes you think Mr. Slayton has anything to do with the missing money?" Joe asked.

Mr. Tobey leaned back in his chair and took up the story. "We're training Dennis Johnson to take over for me when I retire at the end of the year. When Mr. McCain told us about the discrepancy last week, I put Dennis in charge of our own internal investigation."

The president's nephew stood up and paced the room. "As soon as Uncle Malcolm told me about this," he explained, "I decided to do what I could to speed along the investigation. I began by using our computers to run checks on everyone in the accounting department."

"What kind of checks?" Frank inquired.

Johnson stared at him. "Computers are like people," he said quickly. "They love to talk to one another. We used our equipment to find out if anyone here has been depositing lots of money somewhere."

"That sounds like an invasion of privacy to me," Joe spoke up.

"Crooks aren't entitled to any privacy!" Dennis Johnson retorted angrily.

"But a person is presumed innocent until proven guilty," Frank joined in.

"You still haven't said what kind of evidence you have on Alistair," Mr. Drew persisted.

"I'm coming to that," Johnson said, and the nasty tone was back in his voice. "We run a program here called Master Data. It's a way for all the small banks in the area that don't have their own computers to use ours. We give them terminals, and they store their information in our computers. We service twenty banks that way. When we ran a name check through Master Data, we found out that Alistair Slayton has an account with Shoreham City Trust. He must not have known that we time-share with them."

Nancy spoke up. "It certainly isn't illegal to have a bank account!"

"How about if it contains over a million dollars?"

Mr. Drew came to his feet. "I don't believe it!" he exclaimed.

"I didn't either," Mr. Tobey said. "But it's true. Alistair had been like a son to me. And now he goes and does something like this."

"There must be an explanation," Mr. Drew said.

"There is," Dennis Johnson returned. "Your friend is a crook. And I'm going to see that he's put away for a long time."

Mr. Drew ignored the unpleasant young man and spoke to Mr. Tobey. "I'll be representing Mr. Slayton," he said. "And I intend to prove that Alistair couldn't have done this."

"I hope you'll be able to," Mr. Tobey sighed. "Can I do anything to help?"

"Uncle Malcolm!" Johnson scolded.

"I want to conduct my own investigation," Mr. Drew explained. "And I'd like to enlist Nancy and the Hardy boys for this purpose. How about it, Nancy?"

Nancy looked at Frank and Joe, who nodded eagerly.

"Good," Mr. Drew said. "Mr. Tobey, I would appreciate your allowing Nancy and the boys to ask a few questions around here."

"Certainly," the president said. "It's the least I can do."

After saying good-bye, the Hardys and the Drews left Mr. Tobey's office.

"I'd like to go to Shoreham City Trust first," Nancy declared. "We can talk to the people at

River Heights Bank tomorrow."

"Good idea," Mr. Drew agreed. "Why don't I take you home, so you can get your car."

It was cold and snow had begun to fall when the group drove away from the bank.

"This whole thing feels wrong," Mr. Drew said. "I just can't believe it."

"But where would Mr. Slayton have gotten all that money?" Nancy asked.

"It seems to me that if he did steal it, he wouldn't have put it in such an easy spot to trace," Joe said from the back seat.

"Right," Mr. Drew concurred. "It makes no sense at all."

"Besides, two million are still missing," Frank pointed out.

When they got out of the car at the Drew home, the snow was coming down much harder. The young people stood in the drive for a moment and watched a dejected Carson Drew walk into the house.

"I don't think I've ever seen Dad so unhappy," Nancy said, as big snowflakes drifted down to settle like a lace hat on her hair.

"We'll work this out, don't you worry," Frank said.

"Yes!" Joe vowed. "If for no other reason than to make that Johnson character eat his words."

Nancy nodded. "He was rather nasty, wasn't

he? He acted as if he already *had* his uncle's job."

A few moments later, the amateur detectives drove off in Nancy's blue sports sedan. The trip to Shoreham took some time since traffic was slowed down by the wet, slippery roads. But finally, they arrived and asked to see one of the bank's officers.

They were introduced to a slight, balding man named Henry Bender, who ushered them into his office. "What can I do for you?" he asked. "I'll be glad to help River Heights' famous girl detective in any way I can."

Nancy smiled. "We're assisting my father, who is representing Mr. Alistair Slayton in a legal matter," she began. "We understand Mr. Slayton has a large account with your bank."

Mr. Bender nodded. "The police were here already regarding this account," he replied. "I'm afraid I can't tell you any more than I told them. The account was opened a year ago and regular deposits were made—by mail. We never saw Mr. Slayton."

"You must have seen him when he opened the account," Frank pointed out.

Mr. Bender shrugged. "No one remembers. All we have is his name and a post office box number to which we sent his statements."

"Was money ever drawn out of the account?"

Joe inquired.

"No. Never. There were weekly deposits, but no withdrawals."

Further questioning revealed no additional information, so the young people thanked Mr. Bender and left.

"There's no use to go back to the River Heights Bank," Frank said, glancing at his watch. "They'll be closed by the time we get there. We'll have to do it first thing in the morning."

· Nancy nodded. "Hannah will be waiting with dinner," she said.

Joe perked up. "That's music to my ears," he said. "Hannah's as good a cook as Aunt Gertrude."

Frank laughed. "Don't let Aunt Gertrude hear you say that," he quipped. "You know she thinks there's no one quite like her."

"There isn't," Nancy chuckled.

The following morning the Hardys and Nancy got permission to visit the computer room of the River Heights Bank. "Talk to Neil Smith," Mr. Tobey advised. "He's the man who found Alistair Slayton's bank account."

The young detectives took the elevator to the basement, where the computers were housed. They found Neil Smith in a glassed-in room that was full of machines and whirring computer tapes. He was a young man in his twenties with sleek black hair and intense eyes. "Are you supposed to be down here?" he asked suspiciously when the visitors introduced themselves.

"Mr. Tobey sent us," Joe said. "He told us you were the one who discovered the Slayton bank account."

Smith nodded reluctantly. "Mr. Johnson told me to do some checking," he explained. "He had cleared it with the police. I came up with a million-dollar account in the name of Alistair Slayton at Shoreham City Trust. I also did some checking on Slayton's spending habits, but couldn't find out anything of interest. That's all I know."

"And you didn't find the other two million?" Frank asked.

"No."

Nancy spoke up. "Is there a telephone here I could use for a few minutes?"

"Sure. Take the one on my desk," Neil Smith replied. "Dial nine and you'll get an outside line."

Nancy thanked him and went to the phone. She wanted to see if her father, who had gone to the jail, had been able to speak to Mr. Slayton.

Meanwhile, the Hardys continued talking to

the young computer technician.

"Does this equipment contain all your data and files?" Joe asked.

"Yes. The bank runs entirely on the computer."

"Does Mr. Slayton have access to it?" Frank inquired.

"He has a terminal on his desk," Smith answered.

"Would you consider him a computer expert?"

"Not especially."

"How do you figure he could have embezzled that money?" Joe asked.

Neil Smith brightened somewhat, anxious to talk about his field of expertise. "The cash was still in the vault," he said, "but most bank work simply entails moving numbers around—either from one computer to another or one place to another. The easiest thing for Slayton to do would be to catch investment returns coming in and transfer them electronically to his account, instead of listing them as bank assets."

"In other words, he could catch money coming in and put it in his account instead of the bank's?" Frank asked.

"Right."

Nancy came back to the others after making her phone call, shaking her head. "I talked to

Dad," she said. "He said that Mr. Slayton swears he knows nothing of the account at Shoreham City Trust."

"Would it be possible for someone *else* to open an account in the name of Alistair Slayton by breaking into the Shoreham bank's computers and *inserting* an account there?" Joe asked Neil.

"No," the man said quickly.

"Why not?" Nancy inquired.

"Nobody could get into confidential files without the proper password," Smith answered.

"Don't you and the others in this department have access to the master data passwords?" Frank pressed on.

"We only have access to the programs," Smith said. "We can read and print the files for statements and information, but we don't have the password that would allow us to transact business within a given file. That is reserved for the bank itself. And now you'll have to excuse me. I have a lot of work to do."

The snow had continued through the morning, piling up several inches, and Nancy had to drive very carefully on her way home.

When she pulled into the entrance, Hannah Gruen, the Drews' housekeeper, was standing on the porch with two now shovels.

"I could use a couple of strong backs," she

103

called, as Frank and Joe climbed out of the car.

The brothers looked at each other, then grinned mischievously. "Your timing is unbelievable," Joe kidded her. "How long have you been standing there waiting for driveway shovelers?"

"Just long enough to catch you two," Hannah joked back. "I figured I might as well have you work for that wonderful lasagna I'm making for lunch!"

Just then a horn honked from the street. They turned to see Nancy's best friends—George Fayne and her cousin, Bess Marvin—pulling up in front of the house. George was a tall, slim tomboy of a girl who enjoyed her unusual name, while Bess, a pretty blonde, was forever fighting the extra pounds she seemed to gain because of her fondness for desserts. She now rolled down her window.

"Are you ready, Nancy?" she called out.

"For what?" Nancy returned.

"We were going to get our hair cut, remember?"

Nancy slapped her forehead. "With all the excitement, I forgot!"

"That's why we're here," George called from the driver's seat, "to remind you."

Just then the girls saw the Hardys coming down the porch steps, snow shovels in hand.

"Hi, Frank, Joe," Bess called. "Looks as if you're ready to do a job on the driveway."

The boys grimaced. "Hannah says no work, no lasagna," Joe replied.

Nancy stood indecisively for a moment. She put a hand to her hair, and pulled it in front of her eyes. "I suppose I ought to get my hair cut," she mused.

"Well, you'd better," Bess retorted. "Don't you want to be gorgeous for Christmas?"

Nancy laughed and turned to the boys. "Do you mind?"

"Mind what?" Frank asked. "If you get your hair cut?"

"Or if you're not gorgeous for Christmas?" Joe finished.

"You guys . . ." Nancy began.

"Go ahead," Frank said. "It'll take us a while to get the snow cleared anyway."

Nancy smiled. "Okay," she said and walked toward the back door of George's car.

"Oh, Bess," Joe called softly, tossing a snowball lightly in the air. Bess looked, and her eyes became wide.

"Joe Hardy," she called loudly. "Don't you dare throw that, Joe Hardy!"

Joe reared back and threw the frozen missile, while Bess furiously rolled up the window. But it slipped inside just before she got the pane closed, splattering in the front seat.

Frank held another missile in hand and laughed as he watched Bess scolding him through the closed window. He tossed his snowball the moment George drove away. It smashed against the car's side.

"They'll get even with us when they come back, that's for sure," he said, then picked up his shovel. Joe did the same, and soon they were working away. "Did you notice anything funny about that computer guy at the bank?" Joe asked after a moment.

"Neil Smith?" Frank returned. "Hm. He wasn't too happy to talk to us, and even when he did, he thought very carefully about every word."

"You didn't trust him either?"

"Not as far as I could throw him."

Joe stopped working and leaned on his shovel. "Something doesn't make sense to me. He claims that no one could have gotten into the files at the Shoreham bank and added an account unless he knew the password."

"Right."

"Well, how would Mr. Slayton know the password?"

"He wouldn't," Frank responded.

"It doesn't add up," Joe declared. "And what about the missing two million? Why would anyone put a million into an account and hide the other two?"

"Got a theory?" Frank asked.

"I sure do," Joe replied with a grin. "If we don't shovel, we don't eat."

After finishing the driveway, the Hardys went inside to change into dry clothes. When they came back downstairs, Nancy had returned, her hair trimmed nicely. She sat in the comfortable living room talking with her father.

When she saw Frank and Joe, her eyes twinkled. "Bess says she's going to get even with you," she said.

"We figured that." Joe chuckled. "Any news about Mr. Slayton?"

"Not really," Mr. Drew replied. "They're going to charge him with embezzlement, but until they figure out how it was done, they really don't have any case. All they've got is that bank account. And Nancy tells me that no one at Shoreham City Trust remembers opening an account for Alistair."

"Could they convict him just on the bank account?" Joe asked.

"They could try since he can't explain where he got the money."

Frank sat on the floor and looked for the sports page in the paper. "That computer may contain a clue," he said. "I sure wish there were some way we could talk with it."

"That's not impossible," Mr. Drew returned. "I got a call this morning from Mr. Tobey at the

River Heights Bank. He once again offered his help. He's trusted Alistair for so many years that it really bothers him to think he could be so wrong."

"Do you believe he'll let us into the bank's computers?" Joe asked.

"I'll find out," Mr. Drew offered, and stood up.

While he was gone to call the bank president, Joe said, "Even if we get permission to use the computer, how will we know what to do?"

"I have a thought," Nancy spoke up. "On the way to the hairdresser's, I told Bess and George about Mr. Slayton. Bess reminded me that her friend Dave Evans helps run the computer at Emerson College and that he'd probably be happy to help us out."

Frank closed the paper. "This may be our answer," he said excitedly. "If your dad can obtain permission from Mr. Tobey to get into the bank's computer, we'll set something up with Dave right away!"

"Good idea!" Mr. Drew said as he came back into the room. "Malcolm Tobey just gave me the go-ahead. The present password is Moneybag. And here's some other information you may need." He handed the young detectives a piece of paper.

Later that afternoon, Nancy and the boys

plowed through nearly ten inches of snow to Emerson College, which was near River Heights. On the way they discussed their strategy. They parked in front of a building with the words TECHNOLOGY CENTER written on the door.

"Are you sure the school won't object to our plan?" Frank asked as he climbed out of the car and into a large snowdrift.

"Dave cleared it with the administration earlier," Nancy returned. "Since school's not in session right now, the computers are barely in use."

The young detectives trudged through the snow and entered the old, red brick structure.

"Down here," Nancy said, pointing to her left. They descended the stairs to the basement to find Dave waiting for them at the bottom.

"Welcome to the pit," he said and shook hands with the Hardys. Then he gave Nancy a friendly hug.

"We really appreciate this," Frank said.

"Are you kidding?" Dave laughed. "This sounds like the most excitement I'll ever have down here. Follow me."

They walked along a well-lit hallway and entered a metal door marked COMPUTER ROOM. Dave flipped on the light.

He went to a console the size of a typewriter

with a TV-like screen attached. After turning on the power, he began to type on the console keyboard. "I'm waking up the machine," he explained.

Joe took a piece of paper out of his pocket and laid it open on the console. "This is the password to the bank's computer," he offered.

Dave nodded his approval. "That's what we need," he said. Once he had the machine running, he reached beside the console and picked up a telephone. "I'm calling the number on your paper that will connect me with the bank's computer," he explained.

After pushing several buttons, he laid the receiver on a cradle next to the console. The phone and the console started beeping back and forth.

"They're talking," Frank said.

"Just getting acquainted," Dave grinned, "making sure they both know the same language."

After a while, the beeping stopped and the word READY appeared on the screen in front of Dave, who began typing again.

"Now I'm asking for access to their confidential files," he said. The machines typed back and forth for a time until MASTER PASSWORD appeared on the screen.

Dave glanced at the paper and typed: MONEYBAG.

CLEARED FOR ACCESS appeared on the screen within a moment.

"It's yours," the boy said, leaning back in his chair.

Nancy spoke first. "I guess we should start with Alistair Slayton's personnel file," she said. "We'll see what kind of information they have on him."

"Simple enough," Dave said, and keyed in the question. Then he pushed the printer button, and a typewriter full of continuous-feed paper loudly typed out several pages.

He tore the paper off when the machine was through and handed it to Nancy. She and the boys read it quickly.

"Nothing wrong here," Joe said. "A good work record, but Mr. Slayton certainly doesn't make enough money to save a million bucks."

"There's nothing in here about his spending habits," Frank said. "Neil Smith said he couldn't find anything, either."

"Maybe we ought to check out Mr. Smith's spending habits," Joe grumbled.

Dave began typing. "What did you say his first name was?" he asked.

"Neil," Frank said. "But we didn't really mean that you should . . . "

The printer drowned Frank out. When it was through Dave tore the paper off and handed it to Nancy. She smiled.

"There's nothing much about Mr. Smith," she said. "He's only been with the bank a little over a year."

"Odd," Joe remarked. "Mr. Bender at Shoreham City Trust said that the deposits had been going into the Slayton account for a year."

"Look at this!" Nancy said, suddenly pointing to the printout. "What does this mean?"

She showed Dave a notation on the personnel record that said: CLEARED ACCESS TO MASTER DATA.

"It means," Dave said, "that this guy Smith has access to the master data files."

"All of them?" Joe asked.

"Sure," Dave replied.

"He lied to us!" Frank exclaimed. "He told us that he only had access to part of the files and that he couldn't transact business."

"He was pulling your leg," Dave stated. "You either have access or you don't. He's got the passwords. It says it right there."

"Then he would know City Trust's password!" Frank exclaimed excitedly.

Joe tugged on Dave's sleeve. "If we wanted to, could we put a new account into City Trust's computer without actually going to the bank and opening one?"

"Sure," Dave said.

"Then someone at River Heights Bank who had City Trust's password could open an account there through the computer?" Nancy asked.

"Through Master Data," Dave returned.

"So Smith could have framed Mr. Slayton with a million dollars," Joe said, "and cleared two million for himself with no hassles."

"Right," Dave confirmed. "By the way, do they work at night at the bank?"

"I don't think so," Nancy said. "Why?"

Dave looked thoughtful. "Because we're time-sharing with someone else in the same program right now. I had to wait on my access because someone else was clearing at the same time."

"Can you find out what's going on?" Nancy asked.

"Give me a minute," the boy said. "I'll try to crack into the used program."

Everyone waited tensely for several moments, then a smile spread across Dave's face. "I think we've found the problem. At this very moment, someone is pulling out every investment the bank has and is putting them into the money market."

"What does that mean?" Frank asked.

"Well, investments earn money twenty-four hours a day. The bank's investments are put somewhere else overnight, which means someone is earning interest on many millions of dollars." He pointed to the numbers that were scrolling quickly across the screen. "In this case, the Soma Corporation."

"Which *could* be a cover for Smith!" Frank exploded. "No wonder the auditor discovered a discrepancy!"

"It appears that right now a massive effort is underway," Dave said. "My guess is that this guy's trying to make one last big score tonight before purging the entire system to cover his trail."

"What do you mean, purging the system?" Nancy asked.

"He'll get rid of the evidence by erasing the computer's memory of all the transactions," Dave replied. "Seems to me that if you want to catch your crook, you'd better do it fast!"

"I don't think he'll be at the bank," Nancy said. "He's probably safe at home with his own computer, doing the same thing we're doing."

"Right," Joe agreed. "Let's check Smith's personnel file and get his address."

While Dave opened the computer file and then waited for the information, Frank asked, "Is it easy to erase a computer's memory?"

"Yes," Dave returned. "All you do is write the word PURGE and hit the ENTER key. It wipes everything out of memory, then gets rid of the memory itself. Blank slate."

All at once the screen buzzed loudly, then went blank.

"We may be too late," Dave said quietly. "I think it's already been purged."

"Wait," Nancy said, and picked up the receiver to the phone. She listened, then played with the touch tones.

"It's the phone, not the computer," she decided. "It's dead. The storm must have knocked down the lines."

"Oh, great!" Frank groaned. "Now we can't even call the police."

"Let's go to Smith's house," Joe suggested. "We'll call the police on the way when we find a working phone."

They hurriedly put on their coats and went to the door. "Thanks, Dave," Nancy called over her shoulder. "You just may have cracked the case for us."

"All in a day's work," the boy returned with a grin. "I hope you catch that thief!"

"We will!" Joe vowed.

They ran out and bumped into Bess on the stairway. She had just arrived to join the group.

"Leaving so soon?" the plump girl said, disappointed. "I thought I'd be in time to help."

"You are," Nancy said, and quickly told Bess what had happened, then asked her friend to call Police Chief McGinnis and explain what they were planning to do.

"I'll be glad to," Bess answered, and wrote down Smith's address. Then the young people hurried outside. It was dark and snow was still falling, but there were only light flurries now.

Nancy drove to the old section of town where Neil Smith lived. The neighborhood still had electricity, and the street lights were on.

"There," Joe said after a while, pointing to an old frame house. "That's the address."

She parked across the street and the detectives walked to the house.

Cautiously the trio peeked through a crack in the blinds covering a window next to the door.

"He's at the kitchen table," Nancy whispered. "Working on a computer!"

"Now he's taking off the cover," Joe said. "Why do you think he's doing that?"

"I'm not sure," Frank spoke up, "but he could be plugging in an extra disk drive to speed up the erasure. We've got to stop him right away!" With that he went to the front door. It proved to be unlocked.

"Our friend is certainly sure of himself," the boy muttered and walked into the house with the others close behind.

Smith flared around when he heard their footsteps. "What do you want?" he demanded angrily. "Get out of my house!"

"We're making a citizen's arrest!" Frank declared. "Step away from that computer."

Smith looked at the machine, then back at the Hardys. Uncertainly, he stood up.

"That's better," Joe said.

"I don't think so," came a voice from the entrance to the living room.

They turned to see Mr. Tobey's nephew, Dennis Johnson, standing in the doorway. He had a gun in his hand!

"No wonder you were so anxious to convict Mr. Slayton," Nancy accused him. "You wanted to cover up your own crime!"

"It was a good plan until you kids came along," Johnson rasped. "Now I'll have to improvise. Let's see. We can deny everything, purge the system, then say that you kids erased the memory accidentally and are trying to blame us to keep yourselves out of trouble. It'll be your word against ours."

"You'll never make any of that stick," Frank said.

"Why not?" Johnson returned. "Whom will Uncle Malcolm believe? Whom will the police believe? I think it'll work just fine. Now, get away from that computer."

Nancy and the boys stepped aside.

"Go ahead, Neil," Johnson said. "Purge the thing and get it over with."

Smith laughed drily and sat down in front of his console, hands poised on the keyboard, when a loud voice from outside interrupted him.

"Look out!"

Everyone dropped instinctively as a snow-ball whizzed through the open kitchen door. It scored a bull's-eye right on Smith's computer. Since the top had been removed, exposing the wiring of the machine, the wet snow caused a short circuit. The computer crackled, emitting a thin column of smoke!

The boys used the confusion to tackle Johnson and wrestle the gun away from him. Smith jumped up and ran out the back door, followed by Nancy and Bess, who had thrown the snowball. But the girls did not have to go far. The fugitive ran right into the arms of the police. Chief McGinnis and his men had ar-rived just in time.

Soon, everyone was back in Smith's kitchen, where the two prisoners were safely hand-cuffed. The young detectives recounted their story to the chief, who ordered his men to take the embezzlers away. At that moment, Mr. Drew arrived.

"Jones at the desk phoned me and told me you'd be here," he said to Chief McGinnis. "It looks as if you have things well under control."

"We do," the officer smiled, "thanks to these young people. They've done a wonderful thing."

"The credit goes to Bess," Nancy spoke up. "If she hadn't thrown that snowball just in time,

Smith would have purged the system and there would have been no proof to convict him and Johnson, alias the Soma Corporation."

Bess beamed. "I came over right after I spoke to Chief McGinnis. When I saw through the door what was happening, I reached for the closest weapon I could find."

"Well, your aim was perfect—in more ways than one," Joe chimed in.

A moment later the group left the house and walked through the snow toward their cars. Suddenly, something cold hit Joe on the back of the head.

He whirled around and saw Bess standing some distance behind him, her hands on her hips. "Told you I'd get even!" she laughed.

Blond, seventeen-year-old Joe Hardy picked up a CHANCE card and turned it over.

"Take a ride on the Reading," he said proudly, and moved his Monopoly token around to one of the four railroads on the board game. "I'll buy it."

"Oh no!" His older brother, Frank, moaned. "That means you own all the railroads again!"

Joe, Frank and their friend Nancy Drew sat cross-legged on the Hardys' living room floor, playing the popular game. Nancy had her chin in her hands, her elbows resting on her knees.

"He wins every time," the titian-haired girl complained. "Is this why you guys invited me, so you'd have somebody new to beat at Monopoly?"

Just then there was a sharp knock on the front door. "I'll get it!" Frank called so that his Aunt Gertrude could hear him in the kitchen. Then he jumped up to answer the door. The Hardys' friend Chet Morton stood outside. The chubby, round-faced boy seemed agitated.

"Something weird just happened," he said as he followed Frank into the living room.

"What?" Frank asked.

"This," Chet said, holding up an envelope. "A man handed this to me when I got to your house. It's for you, Nancy."

"Me?" Nancy returned. "No one knows I'm here except my family!"

She took the envelope, which had her name printed on the outside.

"I couldn't see his face," Chet said and sat down in a chair. "He was tall and dressed all in black. He wore an overcoat and a slouch hat, even had on sunglasses."

"What did he say?" Frank asked, as Nancy opened the sealed letter.

"He didn't say anything," Chet answered. "He was standing in the bushes by your front porch. When I walked to the door, he came up to me, stuck the note in my hand, then hurried away."

"That's it?" Joe asked, incredulous.

The chubby boy shrugged. "Right. And now he's gone."

Everyone turned his attention to Nancy.

"What does the letter say?" Frank inquired.

Nancy handed it to her friend. "Read for your-self," she said, puzzled.

Frank took the missive and read aloud:

"Nancy Drew:

It is urgent that I meet with you today at 2 P.M. at the phone booth where Meyer's Ridge Road meets the highway. Please be there. It is very important!"

Frank looked up. "It's signed, HB."

"Do you know anyone with the initials HB, Nancy?" Joe asked.

The girl detective shook her head. "No, and I don't know who would get in touch with me here with a letter delivered like that."

Mrs. Hardy and Aunt Gertrude walked into the room, fumbling with purses and keys.

"We're going shopping," the boys' mother announced, "and we'll probably be away most of the afternoon."

Aunt Gertrude spoke up. "I made tuna salad for lunch. When you get through with that, you might try a piece of the Boston cream pie I baked this morning." She eyed Chet's volumin-ous tummy, which betrayed his endless appe-tite.

"We might, at that," Chet remarked with a wide grin, knowing Gertrude Hardy was the best pastry chef in Bayport.

The women went out the front door. As soon as they had closed it behind them, Chet jumped up. "Well, when do we eat?" he cried out.

"Won't your mother miss you for lunch at home?" Nancy teased.

Chet's round face turned red. "I already ate at home," he admitted.

During lunch the group discussed the mysterious letter and planned a course of action.

"I think we should go to the meeting place in two cars," Joe said. "Nancy has hers here. She can drive up to the phone booth, and we'll be a short distance behind."

"I don't think you should go at all," Chet mumbled between mouthfuls of the delicious pie. "It could be dangerous."

"But I want to go," Nancy declared, her curiosity aroused.

"Then let's go early," Frank suggested. "If we get there before our mysterious HB arrives, we may be able to pick up a clue as to what he's up to."

"Good idea," Nancy agreed and looked at Chet. "Do you want to ride with me?"

Chet gulped. "Me?" he replied. "I . . . wish I could, but I've got homework to do."

"On a Saturday afternoon?" Joe asked incredulously.

Chet nodded. "It's a really important project.

I'm way behind." He glanced at the kitchen clock. "In fact, I'd better get home right now so I can get started."

He stood up and went to the door. "Good luck," he said. "I'll call you tonight."

A moment later he was gone.

"Wow!" Frank exclaimed. "Chet was really nervous!"

"How do you know?" Nancy asked.

"Easy," Frank answered. "He didn't finish his dessert!"

Nancy and the boys laughed, then cleaned up the kitchen.

"Tell you the truth," Nancy said, "I'm kind of enjoying this excitement."

"Well, anything's better than letting Joe beat us at Monopoly," Frank agreed.

"When should we leave?" Joe asked.

"Pretty soon," Frank said. "We want a real jump on HB."

Nancy went to the door without hesitation. "I'll follow you," she said, "because I don't really know the way. Just pull over at a spot from where we can see the intersection."

The two cars entered the coast highway just outside Bayport and drove the five miles to Meyer's Ridge Road. There, they turned right and parked half a block up the inclined street, keeping the walk-in booth within plain sight about fifty feet away. Then they waited.

Two o'clock came and went, but no one showed up. Finally, at 2:20, the boys climbed out of their car and walked up to Nancy.

"Looks like a false alarm," Joe said through Nancy's window. "The day didn't turn out as exciting as we thought it would, did it?"

"Let's check out the booth anyway," Nancy suggested.

"Why not?" Frank agreed.

The three walked down the hill to the phone booth. They found a hand-scrawled OUT OF ORDER sign stuck to it.

Frank pushed open the door. He picked up the receiver and got a dial tone. "This phone is working fine," he announced.

"Here!" Nancy said. She bent down and retrieved a small white package from the metal floor. It had the name Nancy Drew handwritten on it.

"It's a video tape!" Frank said, puzzled.

Nancy examined the case. One side was open, and the edge of the cassette could be seen. She handed the package to Joe.

"It's a VHS format," he said. "That means it's compatible with our tape player. We can watch this at home!"

"Our mysterious HB must have come here long before 2 P.M.," Frank said, pulling the OUT

OF ORDER note off the door. "This sign ensured that no one but us would get the tape."

Nancy nodded. "Well, let's go back and play it."

When they left the phone booth, Frank pointed to something on the ground outside. "What's that?"

"A matchbook," Joe said and picked it up. "From the Fisherman's Wharf Restaurant." He opened the cover. "Hey, look at this!" he exclaimed and handed the matchbook to Frank. On the inside the Hardys' telephone number was scrawled in red ink!

"I think we found our first clue," Frank said and put the matchbook in his pocket.

Half an hour later the amateur detectives sat in front of the television in the Hardys' living room. They were waiting for the tape that Joe had inserted into the video recorder to start playing.

Yet, when the picture appeared on the screen, they were more puzzled than they had been before!

"It's just a house," Nancy declared. "A video tape of a house!"

"Maybe something will happen," Frank said. "Let's watch carefully."

But nothing did. They were viewing a fifteen-minute tape showing nothing but an old, two-story brick house photographed from across the street. An occasional car or truck would pass between the camera and the building, but there were no people in the picture. Neither was there any sound except a strange squeaking, which appeared to be a defect in the tape. Just once a jet could be heard passing overhead at a low altitude. Finally, the tape went snowy, indicating the end.

"That's it?" Joe grumbled when he shut off the machine. "What's it supposed to mean?"

"And why was it addressed to Nancy?" Frank added. "The farther we pursue this, the more questions we come up with."

"I don't know about you two," Joe said, and moved toward the front door, "but I'm going to drive to Fisherman's Wharf and see if they can tell me anything."

"Good idea," Frank said, then looked at Nancy. "What do you think?"

"I'd like to work with the tape a little more," she decided. "Maybe there's a clue in it that we missed the first time we watched."

Frank agreed. "I'll stay with you," he said. "There's nothing I can do with Joe that he can't do himself."

Joe waved the matchbook in his hand. "This place is about twenty minutes from here," he said. "I'll call you when I get there."

"Be careful," Nancy warned, as he went out the door.

Frank moved to the VCR and rewound the tape. "Any theories?" he asked the girl detective.

Nancy shook her head. "I'm totally confused. Nobody knows I'm here. I don't know anyone with those initials. Nothing makes sense yet."

"Why don't you call home?" Frank suggested. "Perhaps someone got in touch with your father, and he gave them this address."

"Okay." Nancy went to the phone, but came back disappointed. "No one answered. Hannah must be out. And Dad's not in his office, either."

Frank pushed the button on the VCR. "Let's take another look at this film."

They watched the house again, with occasional traffic the only movement.

"Hold it!" Nancy said suddenly. "Can we go back and look at that truck again?"

"Sure." Frank reversed the tape, then ran it at low speed while the truck was passing. The words BAYPORT MARKET-HOME DELIVERY were written on the side of the vehicle.

"That means the house is probably in Bayport," Frank said. "Bayport Market is a local grocery. I doubt that they deliver out of town."

"What about those airplane noises?" Nancy asked. "They were loud enough to make me think this house is in the flight path—at least at certain times."

"It was a jet, too," Frank said. "The closest airport that handles planes that size would be north of town."

"And from the size of the trees and the architecture of the house, I would judge it to be in an older neighborhood," Nancy added.

"I wish I could figure out that squeaking sound," Frank said, staring into space.

"Run the tape once more, Frank," Nancy coaxed.

They watched the film again, then again. Finally Frank looked nervously at his watch.

"We should have heard from Joe by now," he said.

"I was thinking the same thing," Nancy replied. "Maybe we should call the restaurant. Fisherman's Wharf, wasn't it?"

Frank nodded and walked to the telephone. He looked up the number and dialed. Then he frowned. "It's been disconnected," he said.

"What! Call the operator!" Nancy exclaimed.

Frank spoke to the operator for several minutes, then hung up. "That number's been out of service for over a month," he told Nancy. "And there's no other number available."

"Then where's Joe?"

"That's what I'm going to find out!" He headed for the door.

"You want me to go with you?"

Frank shook his head. "No, better not," he replied. "You stay here in case Joe phones or shows up. I'll call as soon as I know something."

"You want my car?" Nancy asked.

"No. I wouldn't like you stranded here without transportation. I'll have Chet take me."

"Okay," Nancy said. "But be careful."

"You too—keep the doors locked," Frank replied, and was gone.

Nancy realized that she'd said the same warning to Joe before he left. Worried, she sat down and played the tape again, just to have something to do. It gave no further clues.

Fifteen minutes, thirty minutes went by, and there was no word from either Frank or Joe. Nancy went to the kitchen for another piece of Boston cream pie, but found she had no appetite.

Suddenly, the phone rang loudly, making her jump. She grabbed the receiver. "Hello?"

A rasping whisper answered her. "Is this Nancy Drew?"

"Yes. Who is this?" Nancy could not tell if the person on the other end was a man or a woman.

"Your friends are here," the voice whispered. "And you are running out of time."

"Time for what?" Nancy demanded. "Who is this?"

"Another hour, or it will be too late!"

"What is this about?" Nancy demanded. "If you have something to say to me, say it, but leave my friends alone!"

"One more hour until HB," the voice rasped; then the caller hung up.

Nancy held the receiver at arm's length and stared at it.

Frustrated, she hung up and went into the living room. She searched for the note that Chet had given her, but could find neither the letter nor the matchbook. Frank or Joe must have taken them, she thought.

Moving back to the television, she turned the VCR on again and watched intently. If there were any answers to be found, they would have to be on the film!

The house was there, trying to tell her something. But what? She had looked at the place so many times she felt she knew all about it.

It was a quiet neighborhood. She noticed a blue jay flying into the yard and perching on a peach tree in front of the mystery house. The bird walked down the branch and began pecking at a ripe peach, chirping happily as it ate.

Chirping!

That's what the squeaking sound could be—chirping birds! Nancy thought. But there would have to be a lot of them—hundreds!

She jumped up, rushed to the TV set and

turned up the sound. It *could* be birds. "An aviary," Nancy said out loud. "A huge, outdoor cage full of birds!"

Nancy switched off the tape. A large aviary would be a landmark, at least to people who were interested in that sort of thing.

She ran to the phone and picked up the directory. Finding no number for a local birdwatchers' society, she turned to the listing for Bayport Junior College and dialed. When the switchboard operator answered, Nancy asked for the science department.

"Science," a woman said a moment later.

"Is anyone there who could answer a question I have about birds?" Nancy asked.

"Let me connect you with Professor Warren," the woman said. "He's our ornithologist."

The phone buzzed twice, and then a man's voice said, "This is Doctor Warren."

"My name is Nancy Drew," the girl detective introduced herself. "I was told you could answer a question about birds."

"If they flap, I watch them," the man replied in a genial voice. "What can I do for you?"

"Do you know of any aviaries in the Bayport area?"

"The one at the zoo has a fine selection, at least of North American and Canadian species. I . . ."

The zoo, Nancy knew, was not north of Bayport. "How about private aviaries?" she put in.

"Ah," the bird expert returned. "You must be thinking of the Halsey mansion. That's a well-kept cage, a fine addition to a wonderful, old . . ."

"May I ask where it's located, sir?" Nancy persisted as politely as she could in her push for time.

"Out in Heritage Hills, the old section north of the city."

"That's it!" Nancy exclaimed loudly.

"Young lady," Doctor Warren said. "My hearing is just fine."

"Sorry," Nancy replied. "Do you know the address?"

"Oh, I'm sure I . . . let me check." Nancy waited impatiently, listening to the sound of shuffling papers on the other end. Several precious minutes later, Dr. Warren said, "The address is 801 Highland Avenue. Just take the highway north to Greenfield about five miles, then turn off on Highland. Can't miss it."

"Thank you for your time," Nancy said. "Thank you very much."

She hung up and looked at her watch. There were twenty minutes left. She might just make it!

The girl detective scrawled a hurried note about where she was going, then hurried out of the house and drove off.

It seemed to take forever to get to Greenfield, though her watch proved that only fifteen minutes had passed. Once she got there, she turned onto Highland Avenue and drove the three blocks to the address Dr. Warren had given her.

The aviary was there, just as the ornithologist had described it, and across the street stood the mystery house!

She went past it and parked a half block away. Then she walked back cautiously. A chill went down her back when she stood in front of the house. She had come to know it so well in such a short time!

Slowly she moved up to the two-story brick structure, which appeared to be deserted. The sun was just going down behind it, casting deep shadows across the lawn.

Nancy walked around the house once. There was no sign of life. Then she quietly went up the stairs to the front porch. The chirping from the birds across the street seemed to be taking on an eerie quality, and the girl shivered.

She tried the front door. It was unlocked!

She hesitated, then pushed it open and slipped into the dark entryway.

Part of Nancy wanted to turn and run, but then

she thought of Frank and Joe and forced herself to go on. However, she left the front door open behind her in case she had to make a quick getaway.

The entry hall was long and narrow. Silently, the young detective went through it until it opened into a large, dark living room. She took a cautious step inside, when suddenly bright lights came on!

"Surprise!" shouted many voices.

Nancy's mouth fell open. She was standing in the midst of friends and relatives! Frank and Joe were there, with mischievous smiles, as were Mr. and Mrs. Hardy and Aunt Gertrude. Her father was there, her Aunt Eloise from New York, and Hannah. Bess Marvin and her cousin George Fayne had flown in, and Bess was already munching on a piece of the cake that was set out on a big table. Chet and his sister Iola stood next to them. And from the back of the group walked Ned Nickerson, Nancy's special, steady friend!

"Surprise," he said, and gave her a big hug.

"What's going on here?" the young detective cried out.

"A birthday party," her father replied, running up and kissing her on the cheek.

"HB!" Nancy exclaimed.

"Happy Birthday!" everyone said in unison, crowding around to congratulate the delighted girl.

"But—but I didn't tell you it was my birthday!" Nancy said to Frank and Joe. "I didn't want you to feel you had to do something, so I just didn't mention it."

Frank grinned. "Well, you don't have much faith in us as detectives, do you?"

Joe handed her the string of a huge, decorated balloon that reached almost to the ceiling. "We *wanted* to do something special for you," he told her.

"Besides," said Frank, "what better birthday present can you give a sleuth than a mystery to solve?"

"Bess had some doubts about whether or not you'd figure it out in time," George said.

"I did *not*," Bess objected through a mouthful of cookies.

"But I knew you'd make it," George finished.

"This is wonderful!" Nancy cried. "I don't even think I'll be mad at anyone for scaring me half to death. By the way, whose house is this?"

"It belongs to one of my clients," Mr. Hardy replied. "He's out of town for a while and let us use it."

"Then there was *no* mysterious stranger who delivered the note?" Nancy asked.

Chet waved from the crowd. "I invented him."

"And Joe and I photographed the house and planted the tape," Frank added.

"Who made the phone call?"

"I did," Bess replied in the same raspy voice that had alarmed Nancy over the phone.

"Well, you certainly fooled me," Nancy said.

"We only partially fooled you," Mr. Hardy reminded her, and came forward to light the candles. "You *found* us, didn't you?"

"Yes—but—this is the most wonderful birthday I've ever had!" The girl laughed, moving over to hug Ned one more time.

"Blow out the candles, Nancy!" Bess cried excitedly, "and make a wish!"

Nancy was thoughtful. "I wish that everyone could have such a wonderful family and friends," she announced, then took a very deep breath.

They all applauded and spontaneously sang a rousing chorus of "Happy Birthday." When they had finished, Nancy wiped a small tear from the corner of her eye.

A TRAIL OF DIAMONDS

"**S**o, how do I look?" Nancy Drew asked and smiled through several television monitors at her friends Frank and Joe Hardy. The boys stood in the control room of WBAY, Bayport's TV station, which was bustling with activity.

"You look terrific," Frank said through a microphone, watching the pretty, titian-haired girl with admiration.

"I'm a little nervous," Nancy admitted, rolling her eyes. "After all, I'm not interviewed on the twelve o'clock news every day!"

"You'll be fine, Nancy," Melody Page, the program director, spoke up. "Just relax. We'll be on the air in five minutes."

Frank and Joe watched as three cameras were being rolled around the brightly-lighted *Newswatch* set. The director, a pleasant, petite woman who was full of energy, stood up from her chair and joined the boys at the line of several small screens that were set in a long, blinking control panel.

"Thanks for getting Nancy on our show," she said. "The one we did with you two last month was such a success that we were anxious to do another."

Dark-haired Frank, the older of the two brothers, smiled. "She was flattered to be asked, and I'm sure she'll enjoy it."

Joe had been watching the monitors which showed different angles of Nancy. "Which picture is the one we see at home?" he asked Melody Page.

"This one," she replied and pointed at a screen that was slightly larger than the others. "It's called the hardwire. I select which picture comes through it."

"It looks complicated," Joe said with a sigh.

"You get used to it." Melody smiled. Then her expression became serious. "Although it's been a lot more difficult lately."

"How come?" Frank asked.

"We've been bothered with vandalism," the director replied. "The last few weeks strange things have been happening here at the station. We've even had to shut down operations four times."

"Do you have any idea who . . . " Frank started to ask, but was interrupted when the man watching the clock called out Melody's name.

The director sat down at her station and put on

a headset with a mike attached to it. "Thirty seconds," she said.

Frank and Joe looked at the screens and saw a tall, tanned newscaster walk up to Nancy and shake her hand. He clipped a tiny mike to the lapel of his jacket and sat down. Only a coffee table separated his chair from Nancy's.

Melody gave an order through her headset, and a woman began feeding paper onto a treadmill that ran into a small machine. Frank and Joe knew this was what produced the writing seen on home television sets.

"Cue audio," a male voice could be heard, and a band began playing the familiar news theme.

Melody's eyes were roving the monitors. "Number three," she said.

Number three camera was switched into the hardwire. The newsman started to talk as the music faded out.

"Good afternoon, ladies and gentlemen. Welcome to the interview portion of *Newswatch* 8. Later in the program we'll have a film of that blaze that destroyed Waite's Department Store in downtown Bayport and a report on . . ."

Just then the entire studio was plunged into darkness!

"No!" Melody screamed. "Not again!" Then, almost instantly, she calmed down. "Nobody move!" she ordered. "There are too many wires to trip over. Please light matches, everyone."

Small flames began piercing the darkness. Frank and Joe could see Melody shaking her head. She turned in their direction. "Make that five times we've had to shut down operations," she said disgustedly.

Everyone in the control room cautiously walked toward a large sliding garage door that allowed the mobile news unit trucks to get in and out of the building. The door was pushed open, and bright daylight flooded in.

The boys, along with Melody Page, went into the parking lot. Nancy joined them seconds later, her look of disappointment changing to one of curiosity, as they stood gazing at the darkened studio.

"I'm so sorry your television debut was ruined," Melody told Nancy.

The girl smiled sadly. "Maybe they'll be another time," she replied. "But who would do something like this?"

"And why?" Frank added.

The director shrugged. "We have no idea, but it has us all very upset. Once it was a bomb threat, another time a small fire set in a storage room. Each time we've had to shut down."

Just then two squad cars pulled into the lot, and the employees moved aside to let them pass. Private detective Fenton Hardy, the boys' father, was with the police. When he saw the young people, he walked over to them.

"I might have known you'd be here," he said, and winked at the trio. Then his face became serious when Melody Page joined them. "More vandalism?" he asked her.

She nodded. "Right in the middle of the news again."

"It always happens at news time?" Nancy asked.

"Yes," Melody replied.

"Over here!" came a voice from within the building.

They hurried inside to see a uniformed police-man holding a large flashlight, its beam fixed on the wall.

"Somebody cut the power at the source," he declared, and pointed to a bundle of thick gray wires that had been severed at the spot where they led into the circuit box.

"Here," Joe said, and picked up a small pair of lawn clippers from the floor. Thick rubber pad-ding was wrapped around the handle. "This is probably what did the job."

The policeman took the clippers and put them into a plastic evidence bag. "Thanks. That's a good clue."

"We'll check for prints on the blade," Mr.

Hardy said. "But if this is like the other cases, there'll be none. And the padded handle wouldn't show any."

"Well, this is certainly not a case of random destruction," Nancy said.

"No, it's not," Mr. Hardy agreed. "But we can't seem to find a motive either."

"Why would someone want to sabotage a *television station?*" Joe asked.

"I don't know," the policeman spoke up. "And the department is so involved in trying to catch that arsonist who burned down Waite's place that we can't spare enough manpower to do a proper job investigating these incidents."

Nancy and the boys looked at one another. "Do you mind if we give it a try?" Frank asked, rising to the challenge.

"Not if the station doesn't," the officer said.

They all turned to Melody Page, who was staring forlornly at the severed electrical cables. "We wouldn't mind at all," she said. "In fact, we'd welcome your help. It would be a great follow-up to the stories that we've already done on you. What do you need?"

"We'll start by trying to find a motive," Frank said. "If the vandalism always interrupted the news, then maybe there was something on the news that the vandal didn't want shown."

"Do you keep records of what you broadcast every day?" Nancy asked.

Melody Page nodded. "We have log sheets filed on every show," she said. "They're yours for the asking."

"We're asking," Joe said.

An hour later the young detectives were sitting in Nancy's sports sedan at the Bayport Dairy Barn, drinking strawberry milkshakes and trying not to spill any on the computer-printed log sheets in their laps.

"Maybe whoever it was didn't want to see Nancy's interview today," Joe kidded.

Nancy gave him a devastating look, but did not comment.

"Wait," Frank said and held up several pieces of paper. "I think I'm beginning to see a pattern here."

He handed the printouts to Nancy. "There were five big fires in Bayport in the past few weeks—all suspected to be arson," he said. "And every time we had such a fire, the TV station was shut down."

Nancy shuffled through the papers, then gave them to Joe. "That's interesting," she said thoughtfully. "Because each time the studio was vandalized, they couldn't show the film clips of the fire!"

Joe got excited. "That means there must be something on the film that the arsonist didn't want seen on television!" he burst out.

"But what?" Frank asked.

"There's only one way to find out," Nancy said, buckling her seat belt and sticking the key in the ignition. "We'll go back to the station and look at those films."

They hurried to the studio, where Melody Page introduced them to Wiley Sparkman, one of the video technicians, who would show them the tapes of the fires.

Sparkman was tall, with white-blond hair, a nice smile and a generous sprinkling of freckles across his nose.

Joe stifled a laugh as he offered his hand. "You've sure got the perfect name for someone working on an arson case," he quipped, a bit self-consciously.

Wiley laughed. "I know; I thought of that, too. Except I sound more like the arsonist than someone who wants to find him. You know, these incidents have really hurt our morale. I hope these tapes give you something to go on."

He led the group of detectives to the archives. It was a large room, filled floor to ceiling with thousands of video tapes. Sparkman used the marked log sheets to locate the tapes that were made on the days of the fires. Then he put them on a machine he called an editor and copied the pertinent scenes. When he was finished he had all five arson reports on one tape.

"I'll get back to work now," he said. "You can play this tape as many times as you want. Here, let me show you how to use the video machine and monitor screen." He demonstrated the equipment, then added, "Leave the tape on top of the set when you're done, okay?"

"Thanks," the sleuths said in unison.

"My pleasure," Wiley waved and went to the door. Then he looked back. "Just do me a favor, will you?"

"What's that?" Frank asked.

"Catch that guy!" With that the young man left the room.

"We'll try," Frank mumbled and turned to the tape machine. He flipped it on, and they watched the segments. Each ran only a few minutes.

"Five fires," Joe said. "Two department stores, an electronics store, a jewelry shop and a furrier. I didn't notice anything suspicious or peculiar, did you?"

"No," Frank agreed.

"Run them again," Nancy suggested, concentration showing on her face.

"The fires were all early in the morning," Frank mused.

"That means the arsonist could have set everything up during the night," Joe reasoned.

"Maybe he was hired to burn the places down so the owners could collect insurance?" Nancy asked.

Frank shook his head. "I doubt it. Waite's is a

family business. We went to school with Joey Waite. The store did very well and was his father's pride and joy."

"And Micro Chips, the electronics place, is a small branch of a California company," Joe added. "It seems to me there wouldn't be much insurance to collect at this location."

"Run it again," Nancy repeated.

They played the tape a third, then a fourth, time, but could see nothing out of the ordinary. Finally, the detectives were beginning to become discouraged.

"Wait a minute," Nancy said suddenly. "Maybe the telephone company can tell us something."

"What?" Frank looked blank.

"Didn't you notice that telephone van that was at all the fires?" she asked. "They must have been working on the lines."

"Oh!" Frank slapped his forehead. "You're right! I saw it, but thought nothing of it. It *is* rather strange, isn't it. I can't see why they would need a telephone van . . ."

"And what's even more interesting," Nancy added, "is that it was always the same one. The serial number on its side is 3209-S."

"Come on!" Joe urged. "Let's go to the phone company."

Frank looked at his watch. "Their offices are

closed now. It's dinner time, believe it or not!"

Joe grimaced. "Now that you mention it, I'm starved. Aunt Gertrude said something about pot roast and apple pie. . . . "

"We can visit the phone company first thing in the morning," Nancy suggested.

The young people left the video tape as instructed and drove back to the Hardy home.

"What's this I hear about your investigating fires?" Aunt Gertrude demanded in her usual, brusque manner after she served a sumptuous meal. "I thought Nancy was here on vacation?"

"Well, did you hear what happened at the interview?" Frank asked.

"I know, I know. Your father told me," Aunt Gertrude said impatiently. "But I think you should leave the arsonist to the police! This is nothing for you to get involved in."

Nancy smiled. She had been involved in more dangerous cases in her hometown, but she did not contradict the woman, who, under her gruff manner, hid a great affection and admiration for her nephews.

"I'm supposed to go home tomorrow," the girl detective pointed out. "I won't even be able to see the case wrapped up!"

"Sure you will. Just stay a little longer," Joe remarked. "The arsonist seems to strike about once every six days. School doesn't start for another couple of weeks, so you'd be free. It's okay, Dad, isn't it?"

Mr. Hardy smiled. "You know we'd love to have you, Nancy," he said.

The girl nodded slowly, color coming to her face. "I was supposed to go with Ned to the GOOD-BYE SUMMER dance on Saturday . . ."

"Good-bye dance is right," Joe interrupted with a laugh. "Ned knows you can't resist a mystery."

"Just call him up," Frank joined in. "He'll understand."

"Well," Aunt Gertrude said with resignation, "I can see you're headlong into this thing. Just watch your step. Arsonists are dangerous people at best, I should say."

Frank hugged his aunt. "Don't worry, Aunty, we'll be careful."

Bright and early next morning, the three detectives pulled into the parking lot of the Tri-State Phone Company. The building was low and modern, with reflecting glass windows all around. A pleasant receptionist greeted them when they walked into the lobby.

The group told her what they needed to know and she directed them down a brightly-lighted hallway to the office of Mr. Steinway, who was in charge of customer relations. He stood up when they entered.

"Mr. Steinway?" Joe asked, and the man nodded, a smile on his round face.

"Yes. May I help you?"

"I'm Joe Hardy. This is my brother, Frank, and our friend Nancy Drew."

The man's smile widened. "The amateur detectives! I've seen you on television. Have a seat. What brings you to Tri-State?"

"We have a problem you might be able to help us with," Joe said.

"Are you working on a case?" Mr. Steinway inquired.

"Yes," Nancy replied, then came right to the point. "Does the phone company usually send a van to the scene of a fire?"

Mr. Steinway pursed his lips. "Why, no," he answered. "There is no reason to."

"The same Tri-State van was parked at the location of five recent arson fires," Nancy explained.

The man sat up straight. "How do you know that?"

Joe reached into his pocket, pulled out the paper with the serial number of the van and handed it to the man. "We saw the film clips that were made. And this is the number of the van that was present each time."

Mr. Steinway looked at the paper for a minute, then handed it back. "It's not one of ours," he revealed. "Thirty-two oh nine is the call number for the van, but the letter code at the end designates the branch."

"The S?" Joe asked.

The man nodded. "It's a Southport van. You'll have to talk to them."

The young detectives stood up. "Thanks for your time," Nancy said and turned to leave.

"It was nothing. I . . . wait!" the man exclaimed.

They stopped and stared at him curiously. He was rummaging in a large stack of papers on the top of his desk. Finally, he pulled out a sheet and triumphantly held it up.

"Here it is!" he said and gave it to Joe.

Nancy and Frank read over the younger Hardy's shoulder.

"It's a report of a stolen truck!" Frank exploded.

"And its serial number matches the one on the van at the fires!" Nancy added.

"The vehicle was stolen from Southport a couple of months ago," Mr. Steinway explained. "I hope this information is of help to you. Our company might even recover the van!"

"I sure hope so," Frank said. Then the young people said good-bye to Mr. Steinway and left the office.

"Now we'll have to find the connection between the stolen van and the arson," Nancy said as she climbed into the back seat of the Hardys' sports sedan.

"I can't imagine what it would be," Frank said, buckling his seat belt. "Let's drive over to Waite's Department Store and see if we can dig up some clues."

"Good idea," Joe agreed.

The ruins of Waite's store were only a few miles from Tri-State. The young detectives pulled up to the brick shell and saw that the first two floors contained nothing but charred wooden beams. The air still smelled of fire.

"This used to be Aunt Gertrude's favorite shopping place," Joe said. "Now no one will ever get bargains here any more."

"I feel so bad for the Waite family," Frank declared. "This place was their whole life!"

Nancy climbed out of the car, put her hands on her hips and surveyed the damage.

Several firemen were poking around the ruins, making sure the structure was safe and wouldn't collapse until it was torn down.

"Look, there's Dad!" Joe suddenly called out and pointed into the structure.

They hurried over to the famous private investigator, who stood, hands in his pockets, watching the firemen.

"What are you doing here?" Joe asked.

Mr. Hardy idly moved a burned hobby horse with his toe. "Just looking over the dismal scene," he said, "trying to figure out why someone would do something like this. How about you?"

"Checking for clues, of course," Frank replied, and told his father what they had learned at the telephone company.

Mr. Hardy listened attentively. "The police ran a computer check," he said when Frank was finished, "to see if any convicted arsonists in this area have recently been freed from jail."

"Did something turn up?" Joe asked.

Mr. Hardy shook his head.

"Hey!" Nancy called suddenly.

The Hardys turned in her direction. She had wandered from the group and gone farther up the street, to the place where the van had been parked.

Now she was waving her arms excitedly. Something was in her hand.

The Hardys hurried over to her.

"Look what I found," she said, and gave Frank a small blue velvet box.

He opened it carefully, exposing a pair of gold cufflinks.

"It was on the ground, near the spot where that phone company van must have been," Nancy explained.

"The department store's name is written on

the bottom of the box," Mr. Hardy said, after examining the clue. Then he pulled out a plastic evidence bag that he always carried and dropped the cufflinks inside.

"Maybe the fires were started to cover up burglaries!" Frank spoke up excitedly. "The van would be perfect for that purpose. It's enclosed and looks inconspicuous enough. Someone could have robbed the place, set it on fire, then sat in the truck and watched the fun. He probably dropped the cufflinks while he was loading the loot."

"And the whole time, the police would be searching for a firebug instead of a burglar," Mr. Hardy added.

"So what do we do now?" Joe asked.

"We keep looking," Mr. Hardy decided. "Maybe we'll be able to catch this guy before he strikes again."

They turned to the building and stared at the gutted shell that once housed a thriving business. "It's too bad this had to happen," Joe said sadly. "It must have been a terrible blow to the Waites."

The next week passed at a snail's pace. No one was able to uncover any new evidence in the arson cases, but the police had begun to accept the young detectives' theory that the fires were set to cover up robberies.

Nancy did a little shopping for fall school

clothes, but her heart wasn't in it. She was too involved in the search for the arsonist. It was as if the whole town was holding its breath, waiting for the next attack.

On the morning of the sixth day, Nancy and the boys were up and on the street before dawn. As they had done for the last several days, they patrolled the business district, hoping to see the stolen telephone van.

There was very little traffic as they slowly drove along Main Street, just a few blocks away from the scene of the department store fire.

"If something doesn't break soon, I'll . . ." Joe started to say, when his voice caught in his throat. "Look!" he rasped, pointing down a darkened alley.

Frank stopped the car and they all stared. There, parked in the shadows, was a phone company van!

"It's right by the side door of the Ferris Jewelry Store," Frank exclaimed. He switched off the lights and turned down the dark alley, where he parked some distance away from the van.

"Let's see if it's the right one," Joe said quietly and slipped out of the car. The others followed.

Curiously, they sneaked up to the vehicle, which proved to be empty.

"That's it," Joe called in a low tone and pointed to the black serial number, 3209-S.

Nancy had been staring at the door of the jewelry store, which was slightly ajar. A wisp of light-colored smoke was coming through it!

"Look!" she whispered.

"Someone's setting the place on fire!" Joe exploded.

"We've got to stop the arsonist!" Frank declared. He looked at Nancy. "There's a pay phone at the corner. Would you call the police and fire departments and ask them to come right away?"

Nancy nodded. "Be careful when you go in there," she warned, then she ran down the alley.

The boys hurried into the jewelry shop. They could barely see through the haze inside. Suddenly, flames licked around the half-open door to the back room.

The Hardys ran to the other side of the shop and peered into the adjoining room. A pile of cardboard boxes was aflame in the left corner. A man dressed in a black sweater and pants was pouring a large can of gasoline over another heap of cartons and papers farther to the right. The air reeked of smoke.

"Stop!" Joe yelled and hurled himself at the arsonist. He hit the surprised culprit in the midriff, and they rolled to the floor, fighting. At the same time, Frank rushed to the fire and began to stamp it out. But while he worked on the first pile, the second one spread out rapidly, filling the room with acrid, black smoke.

"If it hits the gas, we're done for!" the boy cried, his voice choking with coughs. "Joe, I need help!"

Nancy, meanwhile, had placed her calls for help to the police and fire departments and was hurrying back to the store. As she passed the van, she decided to immobilize it to prevent the arsonist from getting away. She pulled out a pin and used it to open the air valve, slowing bleeding the left rear tire.

In the store, the fire was nearly out of control. Joe had the arsonist pinned to the floor and was about to tie his wrists with his belt, when the man, in one last desperate effort, pulled up his right knee and shoved it into the boy's stomach. Caught off balance, Joe fell over with a groan.

The man jumped up in a flash and ran to the door.

"Help me!" Frank yelled in near panic. Joe decided not to follow the fugitive. He tore off his jacket and used it to beat at the flames.

When the arsonist appeared on the street, Nancy was still working on the back tire of the van. Not enough air had escaped yet, and she realized that the vehicle was still operational.

Quickly, she opened the rear door and slipped inside while the fugitive jumped into the driver's seat and started the engine. A moment later the stolen telephone van screeched out of the alley and down Main Street.

When Nancy had regained her footing, she pulled out her pencil flashlight and shone it around the interior of the enclosed vehicle. On the floor she found boxes with jewelry that the criminal had obviously stolen before setting fire to the shop. There were watches, rings, pendants, bracelets and necklaces—all in lined, velvet containers.

Nancy stared at the treasure for a moment, then she had an idea. She opened the back door just wide enough to drop one of the small cases every once in a while, leaving a trail of jewelry boxes as the fugitive raced through the still empty streets until he came to an old, abandoned warehouse in the harbor area. He drove all the way into the crumbling building, then jumped out of the van and hurried around to open the back door.

He stared in surprise when he came face to face with the young detective. With a muttered curse he grabbed her by the wrist and pulled her out of the van.

"Who are you?" he snapped, "and what are you doing in my truck?"

"Let me go!" Nancy said with all the courage she could muster. "You're in enough trouble already." Her eyes darted around the interior of the warehouse, which was filled with crates and boxes, apparently containing goods stolen during the other fires.

"You don't know the meaning of trouble," the man growled. He was tall and heavyset, and his face was twisted and ugly.

"Give up now and things will go easier for you," Nancy urged, trying to pull her arm free of his grasp.

"It's gonna be easy for me," he sneered. "Once I get rid of you and fence this stuff, I'll be on Easy Street for the rest of my life."

"Thirty to life is more like it!" came a stern voice from behind them.

The man whirled around. In his frenzy he had not heard the police filtering into the building! "How—how did you find me?" he stammered as he let go of Nancy.

"We had some competent help," the officer said curtly, with a quick glance at the girl detective. Then he snapped a pair of handcuffs around the arsonist's wrists.

At that moment Frank and Joe Hardy rushed in. Their faces were black with soot, but they grinned triumphantly.

Nancy hurried over to them. "Did you put out the fire?"

"Yes. We managed to control it before it actually spread to the front part of the store," Frank replied. "The fire department is still there hosing it down."

"Terrific!"

"*You're* terrific," Frank said, holding out a blue velvet watch box. "You left us all these wonderful clues!"

"Your trail of diamonds lured us on," Joe added.

Nancy laughed. "Actually, I took the jewelry out of the boxes. I didn't want to drop them on the street for other people to find."

"That was a good idea," Frank agreed. "Now come on outside. There's a group of reporters waiting for the heroine of the day."

Nancy laughed. "I guess I'll have my interview after all," she said and walked out of the warehouse with a happy Hardy boy on each arm.

DANGER IN THE SKY

Nancy Drew looked out the window of the chartered airliner. The Atlantic Ocean sparkled like a fire opal beneath her.

Frank Hardy, who sat next to her, smiled. "Saying good-bye?" he asked.

Nancy nodded. "It was such a wonderful trip! I almost hate to go home."

Frank agreed. "The water around the Nassau coral reefs is the clearest I've ever seen. It'll make diving in other places seem second rate."

Suddenly, his brother, Joe, who had the aisle seat, poked the young detective in the ribs. "Frank!" he whispered. "That guy who just went by has a gun!"

Alarmed, Nancy and Frank looked up. They saw the man Joe had referred to go to the front of the plane.

"How do you know?" Frank asked.

"He's been walking up and down several times," Joe replied. "He seems to be looking for someone. Just now, his sports coat came open and I saw a gun strapped on his waist."

The flight attendant moved up to them, pushing a serving cart.

"Would you like something to eat?" she asked.

"No, thanks," Frank said. "We had a big seafood lunch before we left Nassau."

Just then the man with the gun walked toward them. He seemed very upset.

"Miss," he said to the stewardess in a low voice, "we have a problem."

"Yes?" she said, straightening.

The man held out an identification card. "My name is Tom Jenkins. I'm with the Justice Department. I've been following a man who got on this flight. But now . . . "

"Yes, sir?"

"He's gone," Jenkins finished.

"Gone?"

"I've searched the entire plane several times and can't find him," the agent confided. "He was here one minute, and the next minute just . . . vanished."

"What do you want me to do?"

"Could you check the cockpit for me, Miss . . ."

"Tully," the stewardess said. "Susan Tully."

"That's the only place I haven't been able to search, Miss Tully," Mr. Jenkins said.

"Certainly," the girl replied, and hurried forward.

"Excuse me," Frank spoke up. "We couldn't help but overhear your problem. I'm Frank Hardy, and these are my brother, Joe, and our friend Nancy Drew. We're amateur detectives. If you need any help, we'll gladly do what we can."

"I appreciate it," Jenkins said and smiled for the first time. "I've heard about you, and may take you up on your offer."

"Could the man have parachuted out?" Nancy asked.

"Not without being seen," Jenkins replied.

"How about the cargo hold?" Joe suggested. "We haven't gotten enough altitude on this Miami jump to lose all the oxygen. He could survive in there."

"No," the agent told him. "There's no connection between the passenger section and the cargo hold."

"Then he *has* to be here," Nancy said.

"That's what I thought," Tom Jenkins replied. "But where?"

Just then Susan Tully came back to them. "He's not in the cockpit," she reported.

"Are you sure the suspect got on the plane, Mr. Jenkins?" Nancy asked.

The government agent nodded. "I watched him go up the stairs. He got on, all right."

"Maybe he disguised himself?" Joe ventured.

"It's possible," Jenkins admitted.

"Suppose I get the passenger list and match the people with the names," Susan offered. "I can go around and say it's a routine check."

"Good idea," Jenkins said. "The man we're looking for is Larry Niven."

The girl nodded and left to get the manifest. As she started to squeeze past her cart, she smiled. "Mr. Jenkins, would you like something to eat?"

The man shook his head. "I grabbed a bite when I checked the galley," he replied. "By the way, call me Tom."

"Okay," Susan said and walked away.

Tom Jenkins looked around to make sure no one else was listening. Then he leaned way down across the seats and lowered his voice. "Larry Niven belongs to an underground organization dedicated to the overthrow of the United States Government."

Nancy stared at him in shock. "A terrorist?"

Jenkins nodded. "He left the country several months ago with a female accomplice, we assume to learn terrorist tactics abroad. Our contacts picked him up in Nassau, where he paid money for a small package."

"What was in the package?" Frank asked.

"We don't know for sure," Tom Jenkins replied, "but we have a suspicion. It could be a triggering device for a nuclear bomb."

Nancy was horrified. "You mean a U.S. citizen would blow up a nuclear bomb in his own country?"

Jenkins nodded sadly. "He's a sick man, and a diabolically clever one."

"Why didn't you arrest him in Nassau?" Joe asked.

"The Justice Department has no jurisdiction abroad. We could only watch him and hope to get him in Miami the second we landed."

"A nuclear bomb," Frank repeated, shaking his head. "Do you have any idea where he might set it off?"

Jenkins looked grim. "The group he belongs to call themselves the 'People's Army.' They've threatened more than once to blow up Washington, D.C."

Nancy and the boys exchanged glances. They knew without saying it that they would do everything they could to stop this maniac.

Susan Tully came back. "I have the manifest," she said, holding up a piece of paper.

Tom Jenkins straightened. "We'll handle it as quietly as possible," he said. "When you make the rounds to serve lunch or pick up the empty trays, ask everyone's name and cross each off the list. Report any odd behavior to me."

He smiled at the young sleuths. "You can start with Joe and Frank Hardy and Nancy Drew."

"What can *we* do?" Frank asked.

"Keep your eyes open," Mr. Jenkins replied. "You'll need every bit of your training in observation to help me solve this."

"I'm nervous," Susan admitted.

Tom Jenkins took her hand. "You'll do fine," he said reassuringly. "Just act naturally."

The girl smiled awkwardly and moved off. Jenkins watched her go, and when he turned back, a look of pain crossed his face. He put a hand to his stomach.

"Are you all right?" Nancy asked.

The man grimaced. "I have a stomach cramp. Must be nerves. This is a big case. I'll be fine in a minute."

He started to walk off, but suddenly he grunted and nearly doubled over. Joe jumped up and grabbed his arm.

Tom Jenkins looked at the young detective. "Maybe it's not just . . . nerves," he said weakly.

"You'd better sit down," Joe said, and helped him into an empty seat.

Susan Tully returned, pushing her cart. Her face was white.

"Any luck?" Jenkins rasped as he held his stomach.

"Not yet," she replied.

"Are you all right?" Joe asked her.

"I'm not . . . feeling well," Susan returned, a hand going to her stomach. "It just came on, I . . ."

"Take it easy," Nancy said, and stood up. She moved past Frank to the flight attendant. "Sit down, Susan. I'll finish up for you." She took the manifest and continued down the aisle. Groans could be heard from several of the other passengers.

"A lot of people are getting sick," Joe said. "What's going on?"

All at once the plane lurched, knocking Joe and Frank against the seats. Nancy fell, and her cart careened down the aisle.

The boys held on to the backrests for balance, as the plane continued to move erratically, rolling back and forth and jerking up and down!

Susan Tully was trying to stand up. "Something's wrong," she said weakly. "I have to get up front."

"Here," Frank said, taking her by the arm. "I'll help you."

She leaned against him for support, and they made their way forward, grabbing seat backs to keep from falling. Several passengers were beginning to panic; others were doubled over, too sick to worry.

"What's happening?" Susan panted.

"It must have been the food," the young detective returned. "That's the only explanation I can come up with. I'm feeling fine; so are Nancy and Joe. We didn't eat. The others did."

"I did, too," Susan said and took a deep breath.

"Are you the only flight attendant on duty?" Frank asked.

"It's not a big plane," she replied, "and only partly booked."

They reached the cockpit, which was separated from the passenger compartment. Susan opened the door, and they walked in. The pilot, a tall man in his fifties, was guiding the plane with one hand and holding his stomach with the other. The copilot was leaning back in his chair, both arms wrapped around his waist.

"Captain Merrit, are you sick, too?" Susan cried out.

"Very," the man answered. "I . . . don't . . . know if I can bring the plane in."

"The passengers are ill, also," Frank said. "Except for a few who haven't eaten. We think it's food poisoning."

"We need help," Captain Merrit declared. "Find someone who can land the aircraft."

"I have a license for small planes," Frank said.

"Good," Captain Merrit replied. "You . . . can take over now." He doubled over with a cramp, then relaxed. "Susan, try to find a commercial pilot for the landing. Maybe one of the passengers qualifies."

The captain stumbled out of his seat, and Frank took over.

Susan staggered outside. She found most of the passengers ill, and those who weren't, were screaming in panic.

Joe rushed up to meet her. "The pilot's sick," she told him. "Frank took over, but we could still use a commercial pilot to bring in the plane."

"Okay," Joe said. "I'll take care of it. You sit down over here." He led her to an empty seat, then went to the intercom. "First I have to calm down the passengers," he said to himself. "And I'd better not announce that we need another pilot. Maybe I can find someone by talking privately to the people who are well." He took the microphone. "Ladies and gentlemen," he said. "Please stay calm. We apparently had a problem with the food and many people became ill, including the pilot. However, we found a replacement for him, so please don't worry. You will arrive safely."

The stopping of the plane's lurching and Joe's reassuring words convinced the passengers that things were not as bad as they had seemed; people quieted down.

Nancy was collecting food trays at the rear of the compartment. Joe went up to her when she pulled into the galley. "We have to talk," he whispered.

"What's happening?" Nancy asked.

"The pilot and copilot are both sick," Joe said. "Frank's at the controls now, but we need an experienced commercial flyer to bring in the plane. Did the passenger list check out?"

"We're minus one person," Nancy reported. "Larry Niven isn't here."

Joe frowned. "Well, first things first. How many passengers are well?"

"Six or eight," Nancy said. "Most people ate."

"We'll have to talk to them. Find out if one of them can fly."

"I'll do it," Nancy offered. "What if we don't find one?"

Joe shrugged. "I think Frank can handle the landing if Captain Merrit guides him. But it would be better if we didn't have to take the chance. Go ahead and talk to the people who are okay, but be casual about it. We don't want to start another panic."

Nancy nodded. "What are you going to do?"

"Search for the terrorist," Joe replied. He slowly made his way toward the front of the plane again, while Nancy approached several people, inquiring what they did for a living and what their hobbies were. She was hoping that someone would mention flying. But she had no luck. Finally, there was only one passenger left, a young blonde woman who was staring out the window.

Nancy bent over to her. "I'm helping out the flight attendant. Can I get you anything?"

The woman gave a deep, throaty chuckle. "No, thanks. After being bounced around like that, I don't think I want to eat or drink for at least three days! I thought those old Navy planes I used to fly had conditioned me for anything. But I really got scared before. What happened?"

Nancy did not reply to the question. Instead, she said eagerly, "You were a Navy pilot?"

The woman nodded. "I flew transport planes for two years."

"Could you fly this plane?" Nancy inquired.

"Sure. But I thought you had another pilot. We've had smooth sailing after that initial trouble."

"We found a passenger who's licensed on small craft," Nancy replied. "But for landing, it would be better to have someone who's experienced with large planes. Do you think you could—"

"Sure," the woman said matter-of-factly. "By the way, my name is Alice Tandy. I'll be glad to go up front and do whatever I can."

"Great!" Nancy said, and led the way to the cockpit. When they arrived, Captain Merrit was groaning in pain, and Frank had no help from the copilot, either.

"I found a pilot," Nancy told her friend.

"Good," the boy replied and moved out of his seat while Nancy introduced Alice Tandy. After a quick handshake he said, "We're Flight Alpha-6. Ground control at Miami International is aware of our problem."

"Okay," Alice said and took his seat. She pulled her purse and a camera case off her shoulder and set them beside her on the floor. Then she put the headphones over her ears.

Nancy left the cockpit, relieved that things were working out all right. She saw Joe in the forward galley and walked up to him. "I've got a pilot," she said. "How about you? Did you have any luck?"

"I found this in the trash," Joe replied and handed her a bottle. It was empty except for a small amount of brownish liquid at the bottom.

Nancy screwed off the top of the bottle and sniffed. It had an odor like strong cough syrup.

"Let me ask Susan if she knows what it is," the girl said.

The flight attendant sat limply in her seat, her face gray and her breathing shallow. Nancy showed her the bottle. "Is that yours?" she asked.

Susan shook her head. "No, I've never seen it before. Where . . . did you find it?" Her voice was strained.

"In the trash can."

"Trash can . . . was empty before the flight," Susan said.

Nancy looked around for Tom Jenkins, the government agent. He was slumped in a seat near the middle of the plane. She walked up to him and showed him the bottle. He had no idea who had discarded it.

"I'm . . . sorry, but I can't help you," Tom whispered. "I . . . feel terrible."

"Don't worry," Joe said. "Everything'll be okay. You just rest."

Since the cockpit had become too crowded with four people, Captain Merrit and his copilot had made their way out and found seats in the front of the plane. Several passengers had noticed it. They began to talk worriedly about the fact that both pilots were ill, and soon caused another wave of unrest. People began to shout, and in a short time, pandemonium reigned on Flight Alpha-6.

Joe went to the intercom again. "Ladies and gentlemen, please listen to me!" the boy said. "We have found qualified replacements for Captain Merrit and his copilot, and there is no reason to worry."

"How do we know they're qualified?" a man yelled.

"Just look around. The plane is stable and has

been for some time. Everything's under control," Joe replied.

There was relieved agreement from the passengers.

"Ground control has been informed of our problem," Joe went on. "For those of you who are not feeling well, professional help will be waiting for you when we land."

This seemed to do the trick. Everyone quieted down and Joe went to Nancy, who was still holding the mysterious bottle in her hand. "Let's check some more," he suggested. "We may have found what caused the food poisoning, but there's still a terrorist on the loose."

In the cockpit, meanwhile, Frank was impressed with Alice Tandy. "You seem to know your way with this bucket pretty well," he said.

The woman smiled. "If you've flown one, you've flown them all. Actually, this baby's in pretty good shape."

Frank noticed her gear on the floor beside the seat. It seemed to be in the way of her left leg. He leaned over to move it for her.

"That's okay," she said. "Leave it. I always like to have my camera close at hand. It's my business, you know. After leaving the Navy I became a freelance photographer."

"Sure," Frank said, settling back in his seat.

"We're coming close," Alice said. "I'm going to take her down a bit. Keep your eyes on the altitude gauge and tell me when we reach six hundred feet."

"Got it," Frank said, watching the numbers slowly count backwards as they began their descent.

Just then a voice crackled through Frank's headset. "Flight A-6, that's Alpha-6, come in please."

Alice Tandy nodded for Frank to take the call. He cleared his throat and spoke into the mouthpiece. "This is Alpha-6. Over."

"This is ground control, Miami International," the voice droned. "You are cleared for emergency landing on runway nine, that's runway zero niner. Do you think you can make it? Over."

Alice nodded. Frank pointed to the altimeter. They had reached six hundred feet.

"That's a roger on runway zero niner," Frank said. "We have leveled off at six hundred feet and will begin our approach shortly. Are medical personnel standing by? Over."

"Roger, Alpha-6. We have ambulances and medical teams waiting. Is there anything else we can do for you? Over."

Frank looked at the woman. She shook her head. "No, thanks, Miami," Frank said. "We just want you to know that we appreciate it. You're lifesavers. Over."

"*You* people are the lifesavers," the crackly voice returned. "And there's enough press waiting here to make you national heroes if you get down safely."

Frank and Alice exchanged smiles. "I'd settle for a hot bath right now," Alice declared.

In the passenger compartment, Joe moved from seat to seat, searching for clues. The more he looked, the more he began to believe that Niven had really vanished.

Dejectedly, the boy sat down in the front section of the plane, which was usually reserved for first-class passengers. Suddenly, he had an idea. When you travel first class, you can store things in a closet, he thought. Perhaps someone could hide in it, too!

Quickly, Joe went to the closet. It did not seem large enough to hold a man, but he opened the door anyway. On the floor stood a pair of men's shoes. A red shirt and a pair of pants lay in a bundle in one corner!

Joe took the clothes, closed the closet and went to Tom Jenkins. The man was still doubled over with cramps, but he perked up slightly when he saw the shirt.

"That's his," he said. "That's his shirt!"

Nancy moved over to them. "What's this?" she asked.

"Niven's shirt," Joe explained. "I found it in the closet."

"That means he's on the plane, probably in disguise!" the girl said excitedly.

"But I thought you said all the passengers checked out okay," Joe said, "with one not accounted for."

"They did," Nancy said, puzzled.

"So that leaves us right where we started," Joe grumbled. "We still have a missing terrorist."

"A missing terrorist without any clothes," Nancy added. "We'd better tell Frank what we found." She and Joe hurried toward the cockpit, where Frank was talking rapidly to Alice Tandy.

"There's the airport!" he said, pointing out the windshield. The tower was now plainly visible in the distance.

"Tell ground control that we're coming in," the woman said.

Frank spoke to the controller. "This is Alpha-6. We have the airport in sight," he said. "Over."

The radio crackled back, "Roger, Alpha-6. All other traffic has been diverted. You may begin your approach when ready. Over."

"Roger," Frank said. "Out."

"Let's take her down," Alice Tandy decided.

Just then Joe and Nancy stuck their heads through the door. "We've found Niven's clothes," Joe told his brother.

"But we don't have *him*," Nancy added. "He

must be in disguise, but we don't have any extra passengers."

Frank tightened his lips. He had promised Tom Jenkins that he would find the terrorist, but now he had to help bring the plane in. "We're going to land," he said, "so we have to worry about that first. Make sure the passengers have their seat belts on, then strap yourselves in."

"Yes," Joe said, and he and Nancy left.

"Here comes the runway," Alice called out. "Get ready."

"I am," Frank said, but he wasn't nearly as sure of himself as he sounded.

"Flaps down," Alice said, pulling a lever. The plane's speed slowed discernibly. And when she reversed the engine thrust, they seemed to be floating.

"Gear down," she went on, checking the indicator light on the panel. "Now we just follow the yellow brick road."

Frank glanced at her. "As long as we don't land in Kansas," he said dryly.

The runway first looked like a ribbon, then a highway. The plane set down, bouncing once or twice. When they were on solid surface, the woman braked hard to slow the aircraft even further.

She had landed with the expertise of a seasoned pilot. Frank didn't know how scared he had been until he uncramped his fingers from the armrest of his seat.

He could see a crowd of people running toward them. There were airport personnel pushing the wheeled stairs that the passengers would debark on. There were medical people and newsmen with TV cameras, all rushing to greet Flight Alpha-6.

"Looks like we'll be on television tonight," Alice Tandy said with a grin.

"You did a great job," Frank complimented her, but his mind was turning toward the terrorist again, who had a triggering mechanism for an atomic bomb!

The cockpit door opened and Joe stuck his head in. Frank could hear the passengers cheering in the background.

"Great landing!" Joe said. "My brother the ace pilot!"

Frank felt himself blush. He unstrapped his seat belt and went to the outside door on the other side of the cockpit partition. Joe was already turning the locking wheel to open it.

The door swung open, and they were greeted by the people waiting for them. Medical personnel in white poured into the plane immediately, carrying folded up stretchers.

Nancy joined Frank and Joe near the doorway. A man in a pin-striped suit walked up to them.

"I'm Doctor Benson from the poison control team at Miami General. Can you give me some indication of what's going on here so we'll know what to look for?"

Nancy handed him the bottle. "We found this in the trash can," she said.

The man held the bottle up to the light, a slight smile coming to his lips. Then he took off the top and smelled it.

"You've been the victims of a monstrous practical joke," he said.

"What do you mean?" Frank asked.

"We don't need to even test this," the doctor returned. "It's ipecac syrup, a substance we use at the poison center to induce nausea in patients who have been poisoned." He shook his head. "It will make you sick as a dog, but it's harmless. It's even sold over the counter at drug stores. If this is what caused all the problems, we don't have to worry. Everyone will be fine in a couple of hours."

Nancy and the boys exchanged glances. "Obviously, someone wanted to get all these people sick," she said. "But why?"

Neither Frank nor Joe had an answer to her question.

Another man in a business suit had entered the plane and was talking to the passengers as they were being carried out. "Don't worry, ladies and gentlemen. We'll take care of everything for you. We'll check your bags through customs so that when you feel better, you can just pick them up."

"Let's get out of the way," Joe suggested. The young detectives stepped out of the plane and went down the stairs.

Alice Tandy was there, talking with a group of reporters. She pointed to Frank.

"There's my co-pilot!" she called out.

"Your public awaits you," Nancy said jokingly.

Frank rolled his eyes, then noticed Tom Jenkins, who lay on a stretcher and was surrounded by several men.

The trio hurried over to him. "I'm sorry," Frank said. "We didn't come through for you."

"It wasn't your fault," Jenkins said, then introduced the young detectives to the men, who were all from the Justice Department.

Everyone shook hands, even though the mood was subdued. The loss of Niven was a hard blow, amidst the jubilation about the rescued flight.

Now newsmen were crowding in on Frank, Alice Tandy tagging along with them.

"How does it feel to be a hero?" one of the reporters asked.

"I didn't do much," Frank returned. "Alice handled everything. I was just backing her up."

The airline spokesman, who had been talking

to the sick passengers on the plane, approached the group. "I want to congratulate these brave people," he said to the reporters, and put an arm around Frank and Alice. "And to show our gratitude, we'll give them a free vacation in Miami that they'll never forget."

"Wow, thanks!" Alice Tandy said. "I really appreciate it."

"No, we're the ones who appreciate it," the man said. "And now, if you'll just come with me, we'll go in the VIP door to avoid customs and get you on your way."

"I guess this is good-bye," Tom Jenkins said, and motioned for the medics to carry him off.

"Wait a minute," Frank said suddenly. "I have something to say that you all might want to hear."

The government agents looked at him curiously, and everyone became quiet.

"I couldn't understand the reason why someone would intentionally poison the passengers on this flight," Frank began. "What possible motivation could there be?"

He turned to Tom Jenkins. "When we discussed the escaped terrorist, Larry Niven, you talked about an accomplice, a woman."

Jenkins nodded. "We lost her trail after she left the country," he said.

Frank went on. "When we realized that Niven

was missing, we examined the manifest and found that all passengers were accounted for, except for one man."

"Correct," Jenkins said.

"Now," Frank continued, "the names are checked off on the passenger list when people board the flight. This proves that Niven had actually gotten on the plane. But what would keep him from appearing and then leaving before the flight took off?"

Joe instantly caught on to what his brother was thinking. "Or an accomplice could have checked in with him and then left, which would explain why we were one passenger short. Niven then put on the clothes of this accomplice . . ."

"We'd better detain all the passengers!" Tom Jenkins urged.

"I don't think that will be necessary," Frank replied. "You see, there was only one reason for the food poisoning on board, and that was to create an emergency situation that would suspend the regular customs and security checks on a flight arriving from abroad. Does Larry Niven have a pilot's license?"

Jenkins nodded weakly. "He's an accomplished flyer."

"And what better way to insure safe passage into a country than by being a hero?" Nancy added.

Everyone looked at Alice Tandy.

"This accusation is insane!" she shrieked.

"Is it?" Frank said. "I bet your camera case contains a triggering device!"

Alice Tandy wheeled around and started running. Her blonde wig flew off her head as she took giant leaps across the field.

"It's Larry Niven!" Tom Jenkins cried out. "Don't let him get away!"

The government agents chased the terrorist and caught him within minutes. They dragged Niven back to the group, and one of them pulled the camera case off the man's shoulder. He handed it to Frank. "You get the honor of opening it," he said.

Frank pulled the top off the case and took out a small electronic box.

"That's it!" Tom Jenkins exclaimed. "We've caught Niven red-handed!"

Frank looked at the reporters, who were busy crossing out the story they had been writing to start a new one. "You came to interview a hero," he told them, "and found a criminal instead."

One of the Justice Department agents put a hand on Frank's shoulder. "No," he said. "We've got our hero, or heroes, I should say. You three have unmasked a dangerous man and made our country a much safer place to live in. In the name of the United States Government, we want to thank you for doing a great job!"